# Emma Lathen

## A Place for Murder Screenplay

"Thatcher is Nero Wolfe with portfolio"

"The American Agatha Christie"

New York Times Book Reviews

# Murder also happens to the rich and mighty, just ask Emma Lathen!

*The New York Times Book Review* calls her "urbane, witty, faultless, delightful." She provides suspense with fascinating insights into businesses and the lives of the rich and powerful. From International to local businesses, where danger and intelligence            go            hand-in-hand.

# 24 John Putnam Thatcher
## Emma Lathen Mysteries

1. Banking on Death 1961. Manufacturing basics.
2. A Place for Murder 1963. Old Rich v Towns People.
3. Accounting for Murder 1964. Accounting.
4. Murder Makes the Wheels Go Round 1966. Cars.
5. Death Shall Overcome 1966. Integration.
6. Murder Against the Grain 1967. Options Trading.
7. A Stitch in Time 1968. Health Care.
8. Come to Dust 1968. Fund Raising.
9. When in Greece 1969. International Business.
10. Murder to Go 1969. Fast Food.
11. Pick Up Sticks 1970. Second Home Developments.
12. Ashes to Ashes 1971. Real Estate Development.
13. The Longer the Thread 1971. Cut & Sew Off Shore
14. Murder Without Icing 1972. Professional Sports.
15. Sweet and Low 1974. Candy Bars & Consumer.
16. By Hook or by Crook 1975. Antique Rugs.
17. Double, Double, Oil and Trouble 1978. Oil.
18. Going for the Gold 1981. Olympics/Amateur Sport.
19. Green Grow the Dollars 1982. Mail Order/Nursery.
20. Something in the Air 1988. Discount Airlines.
21. East is East 1991. International, Robotics & Finance.
22. Right on the Money 1993. Mergers & Acquisitions.
23. Brewing Up a Storm 1996. Beer.
24. A Shark Out of Water 1997. Government Projects.

# 6 Elizabeth & John Putnam Thatcher

## Emma Lathen Mysteries

John Putnam Thatcher reorganizes the Sloan, becomes Chairman, Charlie Trinkam President, Ken Nicolls SVP, Elizabeth Thatcher Head of IT & Venture Capital, Walter Bowman VP of Yes, Everett Gabler VP of No & Maria Corsa, Miss Corsa's niece, a direct report to Elizabeth Thatcher. George Lancer, former Chairman, Brad Withers, former President & Miss Corsa are retired but curious.

The Sloan has automated its branches, moved Corporate HQ to Ireland, set up IT in India, established the VC division in Ireland & Austin, and sold off the Sloan HQ building in New York. The Sloan has gone private with the above active individuals being the major shareholders and become the largest Bank in the World by Capital value.

25. Political Murder 1999. Death of a Senator.

26. Dot Com Murder 2001. Death of a Dot Com Leader.

27. Biking Murder 2005. Death of a Bike Lane Advocate.

28. Nonprofit Murder 2008. Death of a Nonprofit CEO.

29. Union Murder 2010. Death of a Union Leader.

30. Gig Murder. 2016. Death of a Gig Litigant.

# Preface

Henissart and Latsis attended Harvard graduate school back in the day. They discovered they were running out of traditional mysteries to read such as Agatha Christie and Rex Stout. They also learned that most mystery buffs had similar experiences leading to the eternal question: What's next?

At first they were friends and then roommates. Latsis worked in the CIA and spent two years in Rome employed by the UN's Food and Agricultural Organization before returning to Wellesley College to teach Economics. Henissart went to New York to practice law.

In 1960 Henissart took a corporate legal job at Raytheon in Boston and stayed with Latsis during her house hunt. She asked what good mysteries were around and was told there weren't any left.

They then said, "Let's write one." With that they were off and running in their lifetime entrepreneurial writing venture. This reminded me of my old friend Alex Goodwin, now Levitch, the only man I know who has ever changed his last name not to his wife's, bringing me the Umbroller type stroller as a business project and I said, "Let's do it." We did. We were Choate roommates and had gone our separate ways until we had our first taste of organization life for me at General Foods and Alex in law at the US Justice Dept. in DC.

Latsis and Henissart had an unusual relationship for writers but not for entrepreneurial partners. They began each work by first agreeing on the basic structure and major characters; then they wrote alternating chapters. Latsis then composed the first complete draft on yellow pads and produced this edition for Henissart to review. Henissart then typed out the final draft.

They would then get together for a final joint rewrite, eliminating inconsistencies, and synthesizing the work into a coherent whole. Unlike the tradition of a Hemingway and Fitzgerald with an editor like Max Perkins, they jointly did their own editor work as equal partners in their enterprise.

Most mystery buffs have had that moment of running out of acceptable books to read. Each of us can remember vividly the wonderful moment when we found another series to read. This can be your moment with the Emma Lathen series!

I can remember the moment I learned about Sue Grafton, Thomas Perry, Dick Francis, and Emma Lathen herself. Some tap out and get off track like Patricia Cornwell, but they are often terrific while on track.

Being practical as well as talented people, Henissart and Latsis took up the challenge and wrote 31 books together before Latsis died in 1997.

24 were Emma Lathen John Thatcher books and 7 Ben Safford political works written under the name R. G. Dominic. As good entrepreneurs, they let the Safford series go when the John Thatcher series outsold it by a substantial amount.

The series has been extended to six more featuring Thatcher's daughter, Elizabeth, and most of the rest of the cast, this time moving Thatcher up to Chairman, Trinkam President, Nicolls SVP, Elizabeth Head of IT & VC, Bowman VP of Yes, Gabler VP of No, and Miss Corsa's niece on board working for Elizabeth. Lancer, Withers, and Rose Corsa have retired but remain shareholders and are curious as well.

There will be more as The Sloan adapts to the modern world by having moved their HQ to Ireland in a tax inversion, automating its branches to be more mobile and less subject to regulation, centering IT in India, venture capital in Austin, going private, and becoming the largest bank in the world measured by capital value.

Henissart studied law at Harvard after graduating in physics from Mt. Holyoke. Latsis studied economics at Wellesley and Harvard so setting their books in the business world suited both of them. Their seemingly infallible instincts helped them recognize that business people were big mystery readers and could afford to buy a series, exactly what my Aunt Dorothy did.

Martha Henissart chucked when telling me their best book store was on Wall Street itself.

They created the name Emma Lathen out of a combination of letters in their own names, something they had great fun doing. M of Mary and Ma of Martha, and Lat of Latsis and Hen of Henissart. This was reinforced by Emma from Jane Austen. And viola--Emma Lathen was born!

No one troubled to find out who Emma Lathen was for years. The authors kept it quiet to protect Henissart's clients from possible embarrassment.

They created an ensemble of characters to enrich their stories and carry people's knowledge about the Thatcher group from book to book, much like Agatha did to a more limited extent with Hastings and Jap joining Poirot in many books. Emma Lathen anticipated TV series such as Mary Tyler Moore and later Friends that created a cast of characters so we knew them from the beginning of a story and didn't have to labor to learn a new group.

Pure       whipped       cream       without       the       calories.

# Introduction

Emma Lathen used Wall Street, banking, and business as the backdrop for her inspiration for a series of entertaining mysteries. The New York Times said, "John Putnam Thatcher is Nero Wolfe with portfolio." In fact many readers turn to Lathen when they have finished the Nero Wolfe stories. Another New York Times reviewer said, "Emma Lathen is the American Agatha Christie."

An LA review from the Daily News said, "The Agatha Christie of Wall Street."

With those accolades she surely deserves our respect. More personally, she is worthy of reading, especially after you have run out of Wolfe and Christie mysteries.

What is most charming about this 24 book series is that her entourage is in all the books, much like successful TV series such as Friends. Rex Stout had a similar group but they didn't appear in every mystery. Agatha Christie had Captain Hastings, Miss Lemon, and Japp who appeared together occasionally; the TV series got them into more episodes to the delight of Agatha fans.

I was personally introduced to Lathen by my Aunt Dorothy who was a business woman back in the day building houses in Minneapolis and then in World War II moving on to Seattle with her husband to do so. Interestingly, this is the only author my Aunt ever recommended. I have been forever grateful to her for doing so. Much like a Lathen character, my Aunt knew what money was good for and what it wasn't. Uncle Chester and she built houses in the warm six months in Minneapolis and later Seattle, and then took off the other six to enjoy worldwide cruises for the rest of the year.

Her postcards let me follow her from country to country, place to place, as they had a grand old time of it. She was introduced to Lathen in a ship's library with the books bound in lovely yellow sturdy boards produced by Lathen's English publisher. It all seemed to fit; English like Christie; on ship; with business people who could relate to Lathen and her cast of characters.

Emma Lathen was the pseudonym for Martha Henissart and Mary Jane Latsis who wrote 24 adeptly structured detective stories featuring a banker, John Putnam Thatcher, and crack amateur sleuth much like Jane Marple. Thatcher is every bit as endearing and interesting as Poirot and Marple, Nero Wolfe and Archie, and Sue Grafton's Kinsey Millhone, Henry, and company.

Each story starts out with a business/banking motif, points to motives other than money, and winds up with money not emotions being the clue to the solution. Thatcher's clear headed knowledge of money, banking, business, and human foibles is as only bankers can know, leads to his eureka moments, which are always fabulously turned out.

Thatcher's purpose is curiosity coupled with a desire to get his loans and the bank's investments repaid which leads to his delivering killers to the police, signed, sealed, and delivered.

Why was banking as a back drop for these mysteries? Henissart and Latsis put it best, "There is nothing on God's earth a banker can't get into." Voila, and much like their rapier like insights and wits of these charming tough minded authors.

Thatcher was the first fictional detective to come out of the world of business and finance. He became an instant hit on Wall Street and beyond in business and financial circles. This makes him perfect for today's millennial and Z generations so enthusiastic about entrepreneurial life in education, nonprofits, and commercial life, all of which are represented in the work of Emma                                                                 Lathen.

# Cast
## Regulars

**John Putnam Thatcher**, SVP of the Sloan, the Third Largest Bank in the World.

**Charlie Trinkam**, Thatcher's Second in Command in the Trust Department.

**Everett Gabler**, the informal VP of No, who identifies the weaknesses in every situation.

**Walter Bowman**, the informal VP of Yes, who advocates new investment opportunities as the Head of the Sloan Research Department.

**Ken Nicolls**, the budding young banker who operates as an assistant for Thatcher, Trinkam, or Gabler, depending on the circumstance.

**Miss Rose Corsa**, Thatcher's secretary, efficient, and generally unflappable.

**Tom Robichaux**, Investment Banker/promoter, much married, a bon vivant, with conservative proper Quaker Devane as his partner, in the Robichaux & Devane multigeneration boutique investment bank. Thatcher's Harvard College Roommate back in the day.

**George Charles Lancer**, Stately Chairman of the Sloan Board of Directors.

**Lucy Lancer**, the perceptive witty wife of George.

Brad Withers, World Traveler, Sloan President, outside Ambassador, and the nominal boss of John Putnam Thatcher. Husband of Carrie Withers, perceptive upright Yankee lady.

Elizabeth ("Becky") Thatcher, John Putnam Thatcher's second daughter, stunning, smart, and much like his abolitionist grandmother. VP of IT & VC investments.

# Occasional Characters

Professor Cardwell ("Cardy") Carlson, the father-in-law of Laura, Thatcher's oldest daughter. An erudite impractical professor.

Mrs. Agnes Carlson, Laura's mother-in-law who keeps Ben in line and up to form.

Dr. Ben Carlson, Thatcher's son-in-law and Laura's husband. Stays quietly in the background.

Laura Thatcher Carlson, Thatcher's first daughter & family organizer.

Jack Thatcher, youngest of the Thatcher children and much like Tom Robichaux and hence now the junior partner in the firm of Robichaux, Devane & Thatcher.

Sam, Sloan Chauffer known for prompt service, comforting wit, and a warming temperament.

Sheldon, Office boy known for moving equipment, getting Bromo Seltzer for hung over trust officers, and doing other small nefarious chores.

Billings, the sardonic respectful elevator operator known for succinct observations about the day's goings on.

Don Trotman, the Devonshire Doorman and Jack of all Trades onsite.

Albert Nelson, John Putnam Thatcher's man servant and general helper.

Arnie Berman, Waymark-Sims seasoned cigar chomping investment pro.

Claire Todd, Ken Nicolls secretary.

# Characters only in *A Place for Murder*

Gilbert Austin, husband of Brad Withers sister, Olivia Withers Austin, who he is planning to divorce. Works as an engineer in a consulting firm.

Peggy Lindsay, soon to be Peggy Lindsay-Austin, is the candidate to be Gilbert's second wife.

Donald Lindsay, Peggy's free loading brother.

Mrs. Lindsay, mother of the brood and matriarch in the making.

Gilbert "Bud" Austin, Jr., son of the Austins, Harvard Business School student, and Roger and Cynthia Kincaid, Austin farm managers.

Captain Felix Parker of the Connecticut State Police

# Emma Lathen Political Mysteries
## As R. B. Dominic

1. Murder Sunny Side Up 1968. Agriculture.
2. Murder in High Place 1969. Overseas Travelers.
3. There is No Justice 1971. Supreme Court.
4. Epitaph for a Lobbyist 1974. Lobbyists.
5. Murder Out of Commission 1976. Nuke Plants.
6. The Attending Physician 1980. Health Care.
7. Unexpected Developments 1983. Military.

# Tom Walker Mysteries
## Patricia Highsmith Style
## Deaver Brown, Author

01.18. Football & Superbowl.
02.Abduct. Sexual Misconduct.
03.Body. Planned Eliminations for Money.
04.Comfortable. Avoiding Consequences.
05.Death. Wrong Place at the Wrong Time.
06.Enthusiast. Opportunity Murder.
07.Fraud. Taking Your Chances.
08.Greed. Heirs Who Know Better.
09.Heat. Heir Arrogance.

**A similarly popular Simply Media mystery series.**

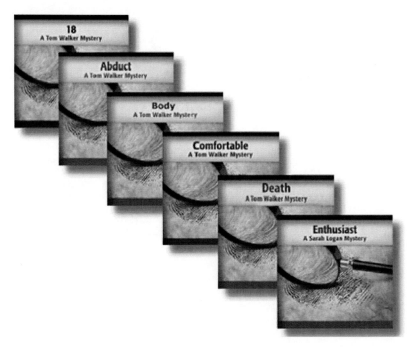

# Financial & Other Facts

Emma Lathen is all about the money not the emotion. In that light:

1. To provide financial incentives for collectors, Simply Media and others savings on groups of 6 eBooks, and the SuperSku (learning from the Star Wars franchise) "all in" collection.

2. Trust that we have all enjoyed this. But as Willie Nelson, Oscar Wilde, and others have said, we aren't above the money. Stay well. And thanks from all of us on the Emma Lathen team.

**Deaver Brown, Publisher & Editor.**
www.simplymedia.com

# A Place for Murder

## 2nd Emma Lathen Mystery

### Ext. Sloan Building-Day

Establishing shot. New York headquarters for the Sloan Guaranty Trust. A modern banking headquarters building, glass, and metal dominates. Use shot from Banking on Death.

### Scene 1: Int.-John Thatcher Office-Day

John Putnam Thatcher (70, handsome, quietly sharp, smart & shrewd), a Wall Street Banker, wears conservative casual business casual attire, and an ironic expression. Everett Gabler (68+, fussy, picky, sharp & usually right) is a long time employee of the Sloan and the cautious VP who finds all the difficulties.

The office is comfortable and somewhat spare with traditional mahogany furniture. No trophies, photos, or clutter. Wide windows. Beyond his office door is Assistant/secretary Miss Corsa's (35, formidable, seems older, a stickler) outside room.


Gabler steps into Thatcher's Office.

Everett Gabler: John, glad I caught you. I'd appreciate a moment if you've got one.

Thatcher: I haven't. My afternoon is taken up.

Gabler steps out; Charlie Trinkam comes in.

Charlie Trinkam (A handsome 40 year old woman): Good. Just been talking to Miss Corsa. Now John, these Handasyde reports.

Thatcher: Charlie, not now. I've got an important appointment. Bring them in tomorrow morning.

Trinkam: OK, but they're important.

Trinkam leaves.

Thatcher (out loud to himself): That's the stuff to give the troops.

Miss Corsa steps in. Thatcher looks a bit wary.

Miss Corsa: Mr. Thatcher, Mr. Gabler and Ms.. Trinkam have both been looking for you. And Mr. Robichaux called . . .

Thatcher: I've already taken care of Gabler and Trinkam.

Thatcher, quietly triumphant.

Won't have time for them this afternoon. Make appointments for them tomorrow—short ones. I'll call Robichaux later. Now Miss Corsa, I want to be undisturbed this afternoon. Have a lot of work to do as you know. Please bring your book in at three-thirty.

Miss Corsa: And

In a show of force,

Mr. Withers would like to see you this afternoon, if not inconvenient.

Her voice was devoid of sarcasm. Thatcher shudders.

Thatcher: Darn! Our President can scarcely be relegated to tomorrow, however richly he may deserve it. I begrudge him nothing but time. But he invariably takes time.

Miss Corsa looks used to ignoring his mutterings. Regards him sympathetically.

I suppose you didn't suggest that I had a good deal . . . no, no, of course not.

Miss Corsa: He did say that it was important. And said he would come down when you got back from lunch.

Thatcher: You know, Miss Corsa, he comes down so I can't escape until he is ready to go.

Miss Corsa looks at him as she would at a dog howling at the moon.

Alright. Call Miss Prettyman (50, alert, shrewd, effective), poor soul, and tell her to have Brad come down.

He pauses sadly, steadies himself, and goes on.

And Miss Corsa, we might as well satisfy Trinkam and Gabler. Tell them I can see them later this afternoon.

Miss Corsa looks at the papers on his desk philosophically, nods, and leaves to call Miss Prettyman. Withers enters with another man who is vaguely familiar.

Brad Withers (Nominally Thatcher's boss; 70; a Yale bulldog and aristocrat; vague; ineffective; does ceremonial duties): John, glad we could join you. You know Gil Austin, don't you?

Thatcher shakes hands with Gilbert Austin (60, a tall handsome man).

Thatcher: Of course.

Gilbert Austin: Good to see you, Thatcher.

Withers (mutters): Helluva thing.

Austin: I asked Brad to call you in, John, because I thought you might help us get this thing moving. We've wasted a lot of time already.

Sees Thatcher's practiced look of polite incomprehension.

Didn't Brad tell you? It's the divorce. Olivia and I are getting a divorce.

Thatcher: Oh.

His a look of surprise and irritation. Recovers. Clears his throat.

I didn't know.

Withers: Didn't mention it to people, Gil. Didn't think you'd want me to, and then I thought—that is to say, I hoped . . .

Austin looks embarrassed not happy.

Austin: I guess not. Well, we're getting a divorce, Olivia and I, and I don't have to tell you that Olivia is being wonderful about it, John. But there's this delay—I'm planning to remarry, you know, and I want to get the property settlement cleared up so that we can get the divorce over with.

Everything is quite clear. Olivia is wonderful about everything—but this little disagreement has arisen . . .

Thatcher: What little disagreement?

Austin flushes.

Austin: Peggy—that's Peggy Lindsay who I'm marrying—seems to feel . . . that is. . . .

Withers steps in and clarifies the point.

Withers: Peggy and Olivia don't agree about the value of the Shaftesbury house. Gil and Olivia have a place ncxt to mine as you know.. Farm and kennels as well. Peggy's a local girl.

Austin looks moderately displeased at this description of his affianced.

She seems to feel that Olivia is being unfair.

Austin: We all agree that Olivia is behaving very well.

Austin is embarrassed again by his personal comment.

But we can't seem to agree about the Shaftesbury place. I thought that if we could get an independent opinion and agree to abide by it, we can get on with the property settlement and the divorce. It's just a formality.

Thatcher recognizes where the safe footing is here and jumps on it.

Thatcher: Certainly. And if you and Olivia are parting, we should review your holdings anyway. If you want us to check your records on the Shaftesbury property, we will. And then we'll get in touch with the lawyers. I see no difficulty.

Austin nods gratefully.

Withers: I hoped we wouldn't, that we could settle this without a lot of formalities.

Thatcher looks slightly impatient.

Austin: God knows, you can't feel worse than I do, Brad.

Said with suppressed violence.

But there's no use waiting. I don't want things dragging on. It's hard enough on all of us. If we can get things moving, we can get the divorce settled. Well, Thatcher, if you'll get the machinery going, I'd appreciate it.

Thatcher becomes matter of fact.

Thatcher: Don't worry, Austin. We'll start this afternoon. After we send somebody up to value the property, you should be able to settle things through the lawyers.

Austin: Thank you both.

He smiles briefly and then strides quickly from the room.

Withers: Terrible thing, this divorce.

Thatcher: Well, it won't be complicated.

Said quickly to avert confidences.

We'll run a review of the trust. Then we'll check the Shaftesbury records and send up an appraiser.. If Olivia isn't raising difficulties, the lawyers shouldn't have too much trouble.

Withers: Olivia is admirable, admirable. She's sticking her heels in about Ridge Road Farm, but I don't say that I blame her. I'm more upset than she is and so is Bud.

Thatcher: Bud?

Withers: Gilbert, Junior. In his first year up at Harvard Business School. We may have a place for him here at the Sloan.

Thatcher pauses to reflect upon another Withers at the Sloan. He shudders.

After 25 years. What on earth has gotten into Gil? He and Olivia have always gotten along. Been proud of her; beautiful home. Dammit, I've always liked Gil. Still do, for that matter, but I simply don't understand this.

Thatcher: He mentioned remarriage.

Withers snorts.

Withers: Remarriage! He's divorcing Olivia to marry that Lindsay girl. Doesn't make sense! Oh, don't misunderstand me. Peggy's a nice enough girl: but compared to Olivia?

Thatcher: I gather.

Realizing he is treading in dangerous waters, he stops and then moves on.

I gather she is younger than Olivia.

Withers: Gil isn't the type to run after a youngster. Peggy Lindsay is younger than Olivia, but that's all. She's plain and she shows dogs. You know the kind. That's how she met Gil. She was showing some of the Austindale Dobermans. Well, I tell you I don't understand the whole thing, John. And besides does Gilbert Austin strike you as the man to lose his head over a woman? Does he even look happy?

Thatcher: No he doesn't. Bear in mind, Brad, youth is often enough; and few of us would look our best while discussing divorce with our brother-in-law.

Withers ignores Thatcher's comments.

Withers: And embarrassing, I don't mind confessing. Then on Sunday we have some damn fool committee meeting about the Dog Show where Gil, Olivia, the Lindsay girl, and half of Shaftesbury will turn up. I tell you, John, Olivia may take all this sort of thing in her stride but it's hell on poor Gil and me, you know.

He stops, and looks keenly at John.

You should look over the Austin place—Ridge Road Farm.

Thatcher had seen this coming.

Thatcher: If the farm is a bone of contention, a professional appraiser is needed.

Withers: No, you could talk to Olivia and Peggy.

Thatcher was chilled by the prospect.

Withers: Then, there's the Shaftesbury Inn. Remarkable woman has taken it over. With a great French Chef, Paul Baudelaire (40, handsome, elegant, a lady killer as well as a great chef). Really, remarkable. Best French cooking in northern Connecticut. There was an article in *The Times* about it.

Thatcher has his back up.

Thatcher: I'm a steak and potatoes man myself.

Withers: John. I don't like to impose on you, but frankly, it would be a big help for me if you could come up for the weekend. Carrie is in the Bahamas, you know, and that leaves me with the whole mess on my hands.

Brad leaves; Nicolls comes in.

Thatcher: I am spending the weekend in Shaftesbury, Connecticut.

Ken Nicolls (28, handsome with beach boy looks in a banker's casual outfit): That sounds extremely pleasant, sir.

Thatcher: I need you to update the Austin holdings, top to bottom on Saturday.

Hits Nicolls like a cannonball. Pauses, and then continues in formal tones. Thatcher reads his mind.

Nicolls: I should get the major provisions of the Austin-Withers portfolio summarized by Saturday afternoon.

Thatcher: Since I am required to spend my weekend in the midst of this divorce, Nicolls, I am not prepared to sympathize with your natural irritation at this disruption of your weekend plans. And if any difficulties arise, you can call me at the Withers place.

And send my apologies to Mrs. Nicolls. How is she?

Nicolls, abashed by this comprehensive right and left, turned fiery red, murmurs something disjointed and flees. Miss Corsa enters as this happens. Notices Thatcher's quizzical look.

Corsa: She's expecting.

Her eyes modestly downcast, when he demanded enlightenment.

Thatcher: Expecting what?

Miss Corsa pivots in outrage.

Corsa: A baby!

Thatcher: Well, the Austin divorce will keep his feet on the ground. But don't let us forget to send a cup.

Miss Corsa sits comfortably with her dictation book waiting.

Corsa: I noted to send the cup 2 months ago.

Thatcher: I should have known. My apologies for suggesting you might not have.

He grins ironically.. She looks disdainful at his friviolity and is not fooled.

Thatcher: Miss Corsa, how would you feel if you had been happily married for 25 years, and your husband left you for a younger woman?

She looks disapproving of this personal comment but gives it consideration.

Corsa: I wouldn't like it.

Thatcher: I thought not. Well, let's see. Dear Sweeney . . . Your letter. . . .

### Scene 2: Int.-Olivia's Living Room-Day

Thatcher: Brad, I am not here to look at Black Angus, as we have for the last two hours. I will be seeing Miss Lindsay shortly. So tell me about the quarrel.

Withers: Talk some sense into her.

Thatcher: I should be thinking of going down to the village, Olivia.

Olivia Austin: Yes. We'll have time for you to look over the kennels and have a drink before you go.

John was crisp and clear.

Thatcher: A drink would be fine. I have been summoned from the comfort of my home to the foothills of the Berkshires to discuss property settlements, not to look at kennels. It would be helpful if somebody gave me some information. Austin Number

One field looks like Withers Number One field. I don't need anymore of that. Now about the quarrel.

No comment from Brad or Olivia. Roger (A small, compactly built man of 45) and Cynthia Kincaid (An attractive woman of about 40) walk in.

Olivia Austin: Oh good. Here's Roger.

Roger Kincaid: Ah, Mr. Thatcher. This is my wife, Cynthia.

They all nod.

What do you think of the dogs, Olivia? We should have a good entry for the Westminster. That last litter is coming along nicely.

Olivia: And a good entry for the local show too.

Roger: Now don't rip me up, Olivia. I've already agreed to go along with you. You'll have your display of hometown spirit. But it still doesn't make sense to waste your big guns on a small show.

Olivia: Of course you're right from a business point of view, Roger. It's just that—

Olivia hesitates with uncharacteristic self-consciousness.

Oh, well, you know how it is. Let's take a look at the kennels now.

Olivia and Roger leave for a moment to go to the Kennels. Cynthia puts Thatcher in the picture.

Cynthia Kincaid: It's the Housatonic Dog Show. It's an outdoor show held someplace different in Connecticut every year. Last Christmas Olivia, Gil, and Peggy Lindsay talked the Shaftesbury Development Committee into inviting the show to

28

be held here. That, of course, was before Gil and Olivia started having trouble.

Now we're all stuck with the situation. Olivia is damned if she'll retreat one inch and is insisting on full participation. Her attitude is that *she* has nothing to be ashamed of. Peggy is the biggest dog handler in New England, so she can't retreat, and Gil is handling the business end. Tomorrow night should be absolute hell.

Thatcher: Tomorrow night? I thought we were having some sort of dinner at the Shaftesbury Inn.

Cynthia Kincaid: We are. The first public meeting of all three of them after the goings on. For the Development Committee Dinner to hear the reports on the show. To make things even worse, the three of them are the only people in town even remotely interested in dogs. Except for Roger and me, of course. We're attending to provide some dilution. I expect that's what you're here for too.

Thatcher takes a Pollyanna tone.

Thatcher: I am looking forward to tomorrow night. I'm told that the Shaftesbury Inn is famous for its dinners.

Cynthia Kincaid: Oh, the *food* will be alright.

With sinister feelings; Thatcher looks at her as a Cassandra. Roger and Olivia re-enter.

Olivia: John will have to hurry off. He has an appointment with Peggy.

Roger: I thought you were from the Sloan.

Olivia: John is handling the property settlement for us.

Roger: But so soon?

With a distressed tone.

Olivia: It had to come some time.

Roger: But you and Gil have hardly had time to try to work things out.

Sounds as distressed as Withers.

Olivia: Gil isn't interested in working things out, Roger. It's his decision, and he's insisting on a quick settlement. Let's not talk about it. . . . What can I get for you?

Thatcher: Then I can approach Miss Lindsay with one card up my sleeve: the side insisting on speed is at a disadvantage. What you need is a leisurely attitude suggesting you are ready to dicker for at least a year.

They sat back with that thought enjoying their drinks.

Olivia: In any event, it's time that somebody lays down the law about this house to Peggy. I'm glad that John is going to do it.

Cynthia: This house?

Olivia: Yes. Having taken my husband, now she wants my house!

Roger Kincaid puts down his drink and shifts unhappily.

Roger: Now Olivia, that's not altogether fair. I know that Peggy is involved in the fuss about the valuation of this house for the property settlement but she's not trying to turn you out. She only . . .

Olivia: Oh, for heaven's sake! Don't be blind, Roger. I know that you're fond of Peggy. I was too before Gil fell in love with her. But that doesn't change the facts.

Thatcher leans forward hopefully at the word "facts."

She's incurably romantic and she has some vision of living here and queening it over the village. Well, she's not going to!

Cynthia: Gil has always loved this house..

Olivia: Gil is very adaptable in his loves.

Roger Kincaid merely shakes his head.

Thatcher: I gather that Gil is willing to accept any agreement that we can reach with Miss Lindsay.

Olivia: Yes and my position is clear. Peggy Lindsay doesn't come into this house except over my dead body!

### Scene 3: Int.-Lindsay Living Room-Day

Peggy Lindsay (A dumpy unattractive woman of 28): I'll die before I let Olivia get away with this. It isn't fair! It's Gil's property and she thinks she can take it away from him by acting like a tragic heroine. Well, I won't let her.

The room is crowded with fringed lamps, gold-framed pictures, small stools, uncomfortable heavy furniture, dark draperies, photographs, mementos, and people.

Mrs. Lindsay (A battle ax of a woman of about 55): Peggy is a dear sweet child. She does not want Gilbert to lose anything because of his marriage.

Peggy Lindsay: Oh, Mother! That's not it. It's just that I can't stand to see Olivia twisting Gil around her little finger. She talks about her home being all that she has left! She looks dark and tragic—and all the time she's trying to cheat him! Can you imagine what it will be like when we're married? She wants to sit up on the hill at the farm with the kennels and have everybody in Shaftesbury saying how well she's behaving! Well, I'm not letting her get away with it!

31

Donald Lindsay (A handsome man without the sneer. 26): Peg's right, you know.

Donald Lindsay is tapping his cigarette holder against an ashtray.

The well known Mrs. Austin just won't admit that she's been licked. Gil is leaving her and it's ridiculous for her to think that she can go on being the great lady of Ridge Road Farm. All that is over.

His mother regards him with admiration. Thatcher inhales happily.

Thatcher: I am afraid that you do not fully understand the nature of a joint tenancy.

He wears them down with a detailed description before delivering his blockbuster.

And of course, if you and Mr. Austin insist upon a judicial separation of the realty, it can be obtained. But, in that case, I think you should reconcile yourself to a considerable delay in the actual divorce.

This provoked a storm.

Donald Lindsay: Don't be a fool! Dig your heels in. You don't have to give in on anything.

Peggy Lindsay: Oh, leave me alone.

Peggy, tears bursting to the surface. They were not attractive tears.

I don't want anything that isn't right. You're trying to turn me into a little schemer. You, none of you understand.

Muffled in a handkerchief, she fled from the room.Thatcher felt no remorse. All in all he was satisfied with round one.

## Scene 4: Int.-Olivia's Living Room-Day

Withers: Sorry to be gone until this morning. Not as happy as you are about negotiation, but it is a good sign you are, John. Tell me, now that you've met Peggy, do you understand this idiocy of Gil's any better?

Thatcher: Not at all.

Withers: We have to go to this damned Founder's Day Parade this afternoon. Here, try some of the ham. Then, there's the Development Committee Dinner tonight and that's going to be pretty dreadful, let me tell you.

Thatcher: I am going out for a walk. Will be back to see Gil in an hour when Olivia is gone.

He returns and sees Gil waiting for him. Gil rises and shakes Thatcher's hand.

Gilbert: Yes, John, put it in the hands of the lawyers.

Thatcher: Admirable Gil. I am going to walk to town and around. Olivia said she would pick me up at the Inn, though I said if she wasn't there I would walk back.

Which he later does and walks back with Roger. Olivia comes back in.

Olivia: John I simply forgot. Will you forgive me? And Roger—thank you! Come in for a drink . . . no? Well, thanks again. And I'll see you this afternoon.

She put an arm into Thatcher's and led him over a few paces to the bar in the living room.

33

Withers: Glad you are both joining me for a drink. Fortifying after all the goings on.

Olivia: John, what must you think of me?

Thatcher: You said you might miss me. Now, I think that you can get me a Scotch.

Thatcher looks forlornly at the unread *New York Times*.

Olivia: So much good advice. You, Roger, Cynthia, and John here, and Bud is driving down this afternoon to tell me what he thinks of his parents' behavior.

Thatcher: As you know Olivia, I saw Gil. He doesn't really seem to care about the property.

Olivia: Ha!

John continues.

Thatcher: About Ridge Road Farm, I feel the best thing to do is to call in a Sloan appraiser and get a firm valuation. Then you can let the lawyers worry it out.

Olivia: Peggy Lindsay is not getting Ridge Road Farm.

Withers: Now, Olivia.

Olivia: Don't 'Now Olivia' me. It's my house, it's where I raised my children, and I intend to keep it.

Thatcher sipped his drink and remained silent.

Withers: But what if the lawyers insist?

Olivia: They won't. She just wants to show me.

Withers: Why should she want to show you?

Olivia: I don't know. I must confess that Peggy Lindsay has surprised me. First, Gil. Then all of this malevolence about the house. After all, I gave her her start.

Thatcher: Start?

With a *double-entendre* in the air.

Olivia: Certainly. She had her first important dog handling assignment at the Austindale Kennels and she's gone on from there. You knew that, didn't you?

Thatcher: Somebody did mention that she was a dog handler. It's not the sort of thing I tend to remember.

Olivia: Well, she's very much in demand. I'd be surprised if she didn't make at least $75,000 a year. You'd remember that, John.

He grins, cheers up.

Thatcher: Indeed I would!

Olivia: Oh, yes, she supports the old lady and that good-for-nothing brother. Well, I'm sorry for her, but she's got Gil and that's enough. She's not stealing my house too.

Withers: Still think you're making a mistake.

Olivia ignored the repetition.

Olivia: Anyway, I haven't apologized enough to John for stranding him that way in the middle of town.

She said turning to Thatcher with imperative appeal. Clearly diversionary tactics were in order.

Thatcher: The walk did me good. Don't give it another thought. Saw the Kincaids. Rather a Cassandra that woman.

Withers: Good people, the Kincaids. Religious family, Cynthia's. It's hard to find good farm managers at a price these days. And Roger's from a Vermont farm, too. Half these fellows don't know a thing about New England farming, you know.

Thatcher: Brad, New England farming has been unprofitable since 1870. I saw the future elsewhere too, though many decades later.

Withers: We jumped at the chance to have them when Cynthia said they weren't taking to life in New York. And we were right.

Yes. It makes a difference having people who fit in to Shaftesbury. Shame we don't have a chance to get in some duck hunting, John. Roger's a fine shot.

> Brad returns to the subject.

And dammit, Olivia, even Roger says there's no point in being stubborn with Peggy about the house if the lawyers . . .

Olivia: If you don't mind, we'll just forget about it for the time being. Bud will no doubt lecture me enough. Tell me, John, are you going down to the parade?

Thatcher: I don't know—are we Brad?

Withers: May be late getting there. If you want to be sure to see it, you might go early. That is, I have to drive into Winsted for the antlers.

Thatcher and Olivia: Antlers?

Withers: Happened to notice the stag's head at the Inn was a little moth-eaten. Got that fine head I shot in Scotland last year. Told Giselle, Madame Dumont (attractive full bodied, 40), that is . . .

Olivia accusingly.

Olivia: Brad!

Her brother, looking shaken, ignores her.

Withers: If you'd care to come along with me, John.

Thatcher: Don't worry about me. I'm going to spend the afternoon reading the papers.

Olivia and Brad look astonished. They leave.

Thatcher (out loud): Clearly, Olivia is in emotional turmoil; Brad is in another of his follies, since comparison of Giselle with Carrie Withers makes the thought inescapable.

The door opens and Gil walks in.

Gilbert Austin: Hello, Thatcher. Escaped the parade and my future in-laws. The usual stuff. Lots of noise; everything's late; people and dogs running around.

Thatcher: Do you know if Peggy has said anything to Brad?

Gilbert Austin: Peggy? No, not to my knowledge. That is, not up until I left for the village anyway. Why?

Thatcher: You know Brad; I just thought he might wade into it.

Gilbert Austin: I don't know, and I don't care.

Thatcher: You don't seem to be having much fun out of this.

Austin: I tell you if I had the nerve, I'd junk the whole thing.

Thatcher brutally.

Thatcher: Well, you don't. So you might as well just grin and bear it. By tomorrow morning it will all be over.

Austin hears a car and looks out the window.

Austin: That's Bud to harangue me. I'll see you later. I'm going out the back way.

Thatcher hears a whiny self-centered self-important voice. Shudders as Bud (an unattractive 22 year old, with a spoiled and whiny expression) comes into the house.

Bud Austin: Roger, he can't do this to us!

Bud enters the house.

Roger: Now, Bud, wait a minute. Don't go off half-cocked. You don't understand.

Bud nods at Thatcher.

Bud Austin: I understand plenty, Roger. Dad never thought of this himself. Oh, what's the use? Leave me alone.

Bud leaves and Roger sits down.

Roger Kincaid: The thing that's really upset him is that Olivia agreed to meet him here and didn't show up. Gil didn't either. Wants to know why his parents are avoiding him.

Thatcher: Not exactly shocking. It is a pity the boy is so young. He scarcely recognizes his parents' plight.

Roger Kincaid: The important thing is to provide some sort of buffer between Bud and his parents at the forthcoming parade and dinner. Things will be bad enough without an adolescent display of prudery. I guess I have to gulp my drink and rush out to be that buffer.

Thatcher: What do you think the latest is I can come, Roger?

Roger grins.

Roger Kincaid: Come about 9 PM. Get a drink and stand in the back. I'll remove your place card. No one will notice with all the goings on.

Thatcher nods with a tip of his glass to Roger. Roger leaves.

## Scene 5: Int.- Bar & Restaurant-Night

Exterior shot of an elegant and typical large New England Country Inn. In the bar John is having a drink while a speaker is braying on in the big room. When her finishes, most people make for the bar there. A few come into the bar. Thatcher nods as Cynthia enters and sits with him.

Cynthia Kincaid: You have to admire Olivia.

Olivia is talking to a depressed looking couple across the room.

Thatcher: Looks like she is depressing them.

Cynthia Kincaid: Well, she's putting on a better show than Gil. I'm surprised at him.

Thatcher: Yes, sitting over there silently with a remarkably forbidding frown on his face But he is sitting next to his son with Bud doing the talking or perhaps more aptly termed, shrieking. Others are noticing Olivia who is being gracious as always, I must admit. And Mrs. Lindsay is displaying Gilbert as a grand trophy. Not a civil engineer's favorite role.

Thatcher chuckles as Cynthia gives him a rather scornful look.

And look over there at Donald getting drunker and drunker, weaker and weaker without Peggy's support. Where is she by the way?

Cynthia Kincaid: Haven't seen her.

Thatcher: We must have some empathy for Gil. He has been outshone by his wife, lectured by his son, made a fool of by his fiancée, dangled as a trophy by his prospective mother-in-law, and toadied by her brother is enough to cast anyone into the dumps. Somebody should declare Gilbert Austin a disaster area and send relief.

Just then Roger arrives in full dinner regalia. He detaches Bud from his father and the party begins to lighten up.

Cynthia Kincaid: Poor Roger. What a day this is turning out to be! We've been in such a stew about the dinner tonight, he forgot about the parade. I just dragged him away from his work without giving him a chance to change. We promised Fanny the parade and he said why didn't I go, which I did; now we've got to turn up and stand by Gil and Olivia and Peggy, too, of course, and so he had to go back and change and now he has to fend off Bud somehow, and if Peggy really doesn't turn up, it's going to be simply ghastly.

Thatcher nodded her off and made for the bar.

Thatcher mutters: It already is ghastly. Nor do I have much sympathy to spare for Kincaid. After all, my employment at the Sloan is involving me in much the same horror as does his at Ridge Road Farm.

Thatcher tries to edge his way toward the fireplace. There stood Bradford Withers with the air of a man trapped in a bargain basement. Thatcher moves towards Brad.

Withers: I can't understand it. I certainly put the antlers on the hall table.

Madame Dumont: No doubt they are somewhere.

Withers: Dammit. I tell you that they're valuable, Giselle. And . . . oh, hello there, John. Didn't see you. Helluva thing.

Thatcher: What is?

Giselle Dumont delivers Withers into his hands with a practiced smile and slides away. Her impressive departure deflected the Sloan's President for a moment.

Withers: Marvelous woman. Marvelous. But women don't understand. Dammit. I made a special trip into Winsted for the antlers and now Giselle says she can't find them.

Olivia glides into the conversation.

Olivia: Brad! Still fussing about the stag?

Withers: Yes, I shot that stag.

Thatcher spots Donald Lindsay and can't resist poking him.

Thatcher: Don't believe I've seen your sister yet this evening.

Gil interrupts and forestalls a need for an answer.

Gilbert Austin: Don, where the hell is Peggy?

Donald Lindsay: She's around somewhere, Gil.

Donald is clearly nervous without Peggy.

Gilbert Austin: What do you mean, somewhere? She's an hour late already.

Donald Lindsay: Now, take it easy, Gil. She came early to fix the place cards, you know. Anyway I saw her things in the hallway. Probably some snafu over flowers or something.

Gilbert Austin: By God, if she's left me to face this mess.

41

Donald Lindsay: Nothing of the sort.

Donald downed his drink in one convulsive gulp.

Thatcher: Young man you'd better pull yourself together.

Lindsay glowers defiantly at Thatcher and retreats.

Mrs. Wrenn: He's drinking too much. That's the trouble with these amateur drinkers. No prudence. Look at Roger Kincaid. He always watches it in public. Sensible man.

Thatcher: Indeed?

Mr. Wrenn: Good for old Roger. Just goes off and has himself a good blowout in private. Drink has been the downfall of many a good man. Don't you agree, sir? By the way, don't believe we've met. The name is Wrenn. And Mrs. Wrenn.

Mrs. Wrenn unresentfully.

Mrs. Wrenn: Nelson, you're sozzled.

Mr. Wrenn: Never.

They go off. Cynthia raises an eyebrow and sits down with Thatcher again.

Thatcher: Mrs. Kincaid, she might wisely look tolerant. Those were real pearls wrapped negligently around her thin neck. In banking you get to know that kind of thing though Trinkam is better at it than I am.

Cynthia Kincaid: I see you got saddled with Donald. He's in a terrible state about Peggy's not showing up! If you ask me, Peggy is fed up with him. I saw her this afternoon and she was simply livid. I have a feeling there's something wrong there.

Roger joins them.

Roger Kincaid: What's wrong where? I've lost track of Bud. Just when that damned kid is ripe for murder.

Cynthia Kincaid: Oh. Well, I was talking about the way Peggy looked this afternoon. When she passed the house, she didn't even say hello. Just walked on, with her head down and her jaw clenched. I thought there had been some sort of fight.

Roger Kincaid: Yes. She stomped past me too. I thought she was out for some sort of row—but good Lord! Even if she's had a real fight with Don she doesn't have any right to stand up Gil this way. It makes him look like a fool.

Bartender: Dinner!

Thatcher let the others leave then stood up. Roger walks in with grin and Thatcher's place card in hand.

Roger Kincaid: John, as you can see, I was able to remove your place card. Walk up to the house and have dinner. Althea has it ready for you. No need to come back.

Thatcher: Thank God!

Roger Kincaid: You deserve a respite and I know this is the greatest bribe I can offer you!

They both grin; John leaves for Olivia's while Kincaid goes back to the dinner.

## Scene 6: Int.-Olivia's Living Room-Night

Thatcher sitting comfortably in the living room, reading a book. Phone rings; Thatcher picks it up.

Olivia Austin (V.O.): John, Roger told me you were there. Come back now. Brad opened a closet door and Peggy was impaled on his famous antlers. Dead. Police here. Brad is trying to get the antlers back; absurd. Get back here now before he makes more of a fool of himself.

Thatcher: On my way.

## Scene 7. Int.-Bar & Restaurant-Night

Thatcher walks into the bar. The same large sprawling place, large enough for everyone to gather. Thatcher nods to the bartender who brings him a brandy.

Thatcher: Drink this Brad and be quiet.

Captain Felix Parker (55; a lifer): Mr. Withers can you join me for a minute? And Mr. Thatcher is it? Why don't you join us too. We'll go in that corner to be visible but not heard.

Thatcher liked the way he approached this.

Thatcher: You did a remarkably quick job of separating the wheat from the chaff, Captain. You have the right people here I think.

Police Chief: Mrs. Austin was remarkably succinct in doing that for us. We know her from her charitable activities. She suggested we include you with Mr. Withers.

The Chief looked at Withers who they also knew evidently, but clearly not as favorably.

Tell us what happened Mr. Withers.

Withers: A coffee pot was turned over and I went over to the closet to help get Giselle a mop and found my antlers on Peggy Lindsay. Unthoughtful of someone.

Chief Parker: How did you know she was dead?

Withers: I can recognize a broken neck. So when can I get my antlers back?

44

Chief Parker: We will see about that. First I want to talk to some others. We have limited it tonight to the Austins, Lindsays, Kincaids, and Madame Dumont.

Nearby Gilbert Austin was heard.

Gilbert Austin: I brought this on her. It's all my fault. It never would have happened but for me.

Parker excuses Withers and Thatcher and asks Olivia Austin to come over. Soon Parker is done with her too.

Withers: He let me stay. That fellow Parker has found out about the divorce. And he keeps asking me about those antlers!

Thatcher: What did you tell him?

Withers: What is there to tell? I went into Winsted to pick them up and got to the Inn around five. There wasn't anybody there so I left them on the hall table. Then I went out and watched the parade.

Thatcher: Did he say anything about how the girl was killed?

Withers: He didn't tell me a thing. But I can recognize a broken neck when I see one I told him.

Olivia told her story clearly, of course, I knew she would but all the same, I thought it best to insist on being present.

Thatcher saw Cynthia Kincaid depart to join her husband with Parker. Soon Cynthia and Roger Kincaid come over to join them.

Cynthia Kincaid: Well, that wasn't so bad.

Roger Kincaid: You did fine. Maybe Peggy was on her way to quarrel with somebody in town.

But Cynthia was pale. She was not enjoying the realization of one of the tragedies she had predicted so freely.

Cynthia: Oh, it's terrible that this could happen! The Captain pressed me as to time I last saw Peggy; I said about 4:30.

Roger Kincaid: I think that's right. And she passed me about ten minutes later. That means she must have got into town just before the parade started, if she walked all the way.

Cynthia Kincaid: We didn't pass her on the road so probably somebody gave her a lift.

Roger Kincaid: I told Parker that I came back and advised Bud to wait until after the parade. But I had to tell him that Bud went off anyway. Isn't Parker keeping Gil over there for a long time?

Austin came over to the group then. The Captain waved Thatcher over again.

Captain Parker: Tell me what happened this weekend, Mr. Thatcher.

He did.

So you can't swear to the movements of any one of these people during the entire parade because you were up at the house?

Thatcher: That's right, Captain.

They nodded to each other and Thatcher got up to be replaced by Donald Lindsay. Thatcher set next to Giselle.

Giselle Dumont: I have been talking to poor Gilbert. He cannot stop reproaching himself for one moment. It is torture for him. And these police they do nothing but ask him if he has an alibi.

Thatcher: Well, does he?

Giselle Dumont: But, no! How could he? He was in his room until the parade. Then he was with the crowd. In movement, you understand.

Thatcher: I understand; avoiding his son.

Bradford Withers was recalled to the Captain. After a few minutes Withers returns to the group and speaks at large.

Withers: Do you know what that poisonous little twerp Donald has told Parker? He says he dropped his sister off at my place this afternoon. That she wanted to talk to me about the property settlement.

Thatcher cut in sharply

Thatcher: What time?

Withers: Four, but, I tell you, she wasn't there!

Thatcher: Brad, sit down and be quiet and let me think. That leaves 4 PM to 4:30 PM open.

Parker strides over.

Captain Parker: All right. I think we've finished our preliminary work here. Not that we've gotten much information from you. You may as well know what you'll read in the papers tomorrow. Peggy Lindsay was killed by a blow on the temple hard enough to break her neck. We don't know what she was hit with. It could have been a fist or a soft weapon. We don't know what the hell she was doing with those antlers. We do know that it was sometime between four and six, medically speaking. The Inn was empty between five and five-thirty when Mr. Lindsay here arrived looking for his sister. Nobody admits being in the Inn during that time. Miss Lindsay was last seen around four to four-thirty, give or take ten minutes, on Ridge Road. She arrived and started putting out place cards. The flowers she never got to. Presumably at some time during these two chores, she was murdered. At that time the parade was going on and you were all out front watching it. At least that's your story. None of you has got a good solid alibi.

He pauses for comment; no one does so; he continues.

Needless to say, we'll do a lot more work. Maybe after we've talked to more of the townspeople some of you will have an alibi. But, by your own account, most of you were drifting around from place to place. I don't think we can accomplish anything more tonight. My man will take your phone numbers and we can call it a night.

Madame Dumont continues over at her table.

Madame Dumont: See poor Gilbert. I feel for him. She is not behaving well, this Olivia Austin. He is absolutely miserable, afraid to approach her. And will she say one word to him? No. She is cold and unfeeling, that one.

Thatcher: I doubt she is even aware of Gil. She is in shock.

Madame Dumont: Then she ought to be. What right does she have to wrap herself up in this iciness, even if she is shocked? He needs her, that should be enough. So he has had this little *affaire*. What difference? It is the way of husbands. It should not be allowed to interfere with one's domestic comfort, *bien*?

Thatcher: Now, if someone is behaving badly, it's Donald Lindsay.

Madame Dumont: Donald? But he has suffered a great loss!

Thatcher: You can't tell me he was that attached to his sister. That young man isn't fond of anybody but himself.

Madame Dumont: But, precisely. And he has been living on Peggy for over five years. And he expected to live on her at a much higher level once she was married to Gilbert. And now all that has come to nothing.

Thatcher: And the mother. The same?

Madame Dumont: Of course. You, all of you, have a very romantic conception of Peggy. It is because you view her in the light of all this tumult about Gilbert's divorce. You see her as 'the other woman.' To Mrs. Lindsay and to Donald, she was something much more fundamental. She was the breadwinner. Poor Peggy! It is not easy for a woman to carry that role gracefully. And she had not the slightest notion of how to do so. She was not stupid, you understand. No woman is who makes that much money in business is. But she could not reconcile that with being the daughter in her mother's house. So she was gauche and awkward and didn't know how to refuse her mother or brother—but there, I think she may have been learning. So sad.

Chief Parker: Things would be a lot simpler, Madame Dumont, if you hadn't sent everybody out to watch that damned parade.

Madame Dumont: Bah. When are your men going to be out so that we can clean up?

Chief Parker: Madame Dumont, this is a murder investigation.

Madame Dumont: That, I already know.

Chief Parker: Would your staff have noticed anything unusual in the Inn when they returned from the parade?

Madame Dumont: Naturally they would notice anything big.

Chief Parker: The antlers.

Madame Dumont: For the fifth time, it is impossible that anybody should overlook that huge object if it had been in the front hall at six o'clock. Therefore—it was not.

Chief Parker: All right. We'll assume that the murderer did a good job of tidying things up.

Withers interrupts.

Withers: Probably some tramp.

Chief Parker continues: ...not that there was much beside the body and the antlers. I don't think that we'll get anything more done tonight. You can go home. But I expect that you'll be available for interrogation tomorrow.

Thatcher: Captain. Do you require me?

Chief Parker: Don't think so, Mr. Thatcher. You mean you want to go back to New York?

Thatcher nodded. The Chief nods back.

Thatcher: Thanks.

## Scene 8: Int-Thatcher's Office-Day

Lincoln Hauser (40ish PR man): I look on it as a challenge, old boy.

Thatcher: Do you?

Hauser: Certainly. It's all in the way you handle it. Why, with the right treatment, we can present a picture of Withers as a man pilloried by the police because of his name and position. In fact, that's just the line to take. A vicious assault on the financial community! Isn't there some town in Connecticut with a socialist mayor?

Thatcher: I doubt if it's Shaftesbury.

Hauser: Never mind. We can work it in all the same. The thing you don't realize is that this is our big chance.

Thatcher: Your big chance to do what?

Hauser: To prove the importance of a flexible PR program. You know we've had a lot of trouble getting the Board to take a modern view of the role of publicity. They think a bank can operate back in the nineteenth century.

Thatcher: That must be very irksome. And of course not provide a VP role.

Hauser grimaces; Thatcher treats himself to a grin.

Hauser: Well, well. These little differences have to be forgotten at a time like this. I've got to be getting back to my office. Things will be humming by this afternoon. A press conference around four, I think, and releases to get out. Pictures probably, and the boys may want an interview with you. We'll have to think about that and—

Thatcher: What I really asked you to stop by for, Hauser, was to tell you that . . .

Hauser: Call me Link. Everybody does.

Thatcher: To tell you that the Board had a meeting this morning and decided on a minimum of publicity.

Hauser: A minimum!

Thatcher: That's right. No conferences, no pictures, no interviews. You're to see to it that there's a minimum of coverage. They have, however, prepared a release which you may wish to examine before distributing to the papers.

His tone made it clear that the examination did not include any rights of revision.

Hauser: But look here, old man, this is sheer insanity. What you want to do is whip up public opinion in favor of Withers.

You've got to make him look like a victim. Now that's not easy with a bank President but with the . . .

Thatcher interrupts ruthlessly.

Thatcher: I think you may not understand the position in Shaftesbury. Withers is not on trial for first-degree murder. In company with about ten other people he has been asked to keep himself available for further questioning. He is being treated as if he were an important witness who was previously acquainted with the victim. That's all.

Thatcher finally evicts Hauser. Nicolls entrance helps with that. Thatcher smiles at him accordingly.

Thatcher: That man is a mental deficient.

Nicolls preserves the inscrutable expression appropriate for juniors receiving indiscreet confidences.

Nicolls: You said you'd want to review the Austin holdings first thing on Monday morning, Mr. Thatcher. I was in here at nine but Miss Corsa said you were unavailable.

Subordinates have their own way of conveying reproach, and it is quite as effective as any devised by their seniors. Thatcher sighs heavily.

Thatcher: There was an unexpected Board meeting this morning. I should have had Miss Corsa warn you.

Satisfied, Nicolls continues.

Nicolls: I think I've got everything you'll want. And the division shouldn't be much of a problem. They don't hold as much jointly as I thought. Except for the . . .

Thatcher smiles; with Nicolls mollified, things seem back in balance. Thatcher says gently.

Thatcher: I can see that you worked very hard this weekend.

Nicolls: Oh, that's alright, sir. I got it all done by Saturday afternoon. Now, if you'll just glance at this schedule.

The folder is proffered invitingly.

Thatcher: I'm afraid I have a blow for you.

Nicolls: Sir?

Thatcher: There will be no immediate need for a property settlement. The 'other woman' was murdered yesterday.

Nicolls: All of that work wasted!

Thatcher: Instead of feeling sorry for yourself, you might spare a little sympathy for the victim.

Nicolls: Yes, of course, sir. Are the Austins still going to get a divorce?

Thatcher: I have no idea. I doubt if they have given the matter any thought.

Nicolls brightens.

Nicolls: Well, I'll file it. You never can tell.

Thatcher is amused.

Thatcher: A very good principle to work on. Although a little callous in this instance, perhaps. But they don't need to know about it.

Thatcher gives him a brief synopsis of the situation.

Nicolls: What was she like?

Thatcher: Quiet, plain, and unsophisticated. Not at all the kind of woman you expect to be a murder victim or, for that matter, to take a rich, handsome man of 55 away from his wife.

Nicolls: Rich is right.

Thatcher: Ah, the portfolio was impressive, was it?

Nicolls: Very. So is Mrs. Austin's. I didn't realize she was so well off in her own right.

Thatcher: She is, after all, Bradford Withers' sister. And, while we're on the subject of Withers, please bear in mind that our official position is that he is not a murderer. With the sole exception, apparently, of the Sloan's PR department.

Nicolls: You mean there's some question of it, sir?

Thatcher: No, I don't mean that. I do mean that between his antlers, which will undoubtedly capture the imagination of the tabloids, and his messing up the body in a momentary panic, there is going to be a good deal of notoriety for a few days. With luck it will all blow over.

He was in shock. Between discovering that he had been unintentionally dragging a carcass around and the sight of the body itself, one arm was pretty badly mangled by the antlers, and having everything he did just entangle that mass of blood, tweed, and horns more firmly, he lost his head. Thank heavens he seems to have regained some control now. He was doing fine this morning. Having to stand by his sister helps. She and her husband are worried about the publicity.

Nicolls: The Austins don't go in for that sort of thing?

Thatcher: Most emphatically not.

Nicolls: Well when you go in for messy divorces, you have to be prepared to wash your dirty linen in public. Marriage entails a good deal of responsibility.

Thatcher clicks, the baby Miss Corsa talked about.

Thatcher: A commendable point of view, Nicolls. But in this case I wouldn't be surprised if they get the notoriety without getting the divorce.

Nicolls: Then in that case I have done a lot of work for nothing.

With a bit of a whine.

Thatcher: It won't be the last time that happens to you. And while we're on the subject of work. One job is to attend a stockholders' meeting for Michigan Motors. It never hurts to let them know we're keeping an eye on things.

Nicolls: How should I vote the things?

Thatcher: For management, of course. But do it at the last possible moment. And look very, very grave. Go off and practice being grave.

Nicolls leaves; Thatcher strides out to lunch with Robichaux.

### Scene 9: Int.-NYC Bar & Restaurant-Day

Robichaux: We'll let the Sloan in on the ground floor. There isn't going to be any trouble moving this issue. Everybody on the Street wants a piece.

Thatcher looks skeptical.

Thatcher: The last time you let the Sloan in on the ground floor was with Stevenson Can. It fell nine points and stayed there as if it had been frozen.

Robichaux: Now, Putt, why bring that up? Stevenson was a mistake. We all admit that. But this drug house is different. Wait until you see their earnings history.

Financial statements are flourished.

Thatcher: Tom, I guess you have hoodwinked me again. I'll turn Bowman's research people loose; what he doesn't find is usually not worth finding. And he weighed in against Stevenson Can as I recall.

Grinning.

Robichaux: OK, have your fun.

Thatcher: Expensive fun, Tom.

Robichaux: By the way, I hear that girl who was breaking up Gil Austin's home got herself murdered. Francis is in a great taking about the whole thing. Says he'd offer to run up to Shaftesbury and stand by but he doesn't know to whom he should make the offer—Gil or Olivia.

Thatcher: Francis? You mean Devane? Your partner? What does he have to do with the Austins? I didn't even know that *you* or he knew them.

Robichaux: Oh, sure. Gil and Francis are both from Philadelphia. They're bigwigs in the American Friends Service Committee. Always getting together to send relief to some place like the Congo. In fact I think that's how they met. Francis, you know, was a great little ambulance driver in his youth. Libya, China, all sorts of hellholes. Of course, he's given up that sort of thing now.

Thatcher: Tom, you have always been mildly defensive of your partner's disreputable past of good works, though boasting of your own time in a succession of impeccable night spots. Do you know Olivia too?

Robichaux: Known her for years. Really know her much better than Gil. She and Tessie used to patroness at balls and charity do's together. My third wife. You remember, Tessie was great for patronessing.

Thatcher: Tom, as usual, I remember nothing of the sort. She must have slipped in and out of your life without leaving a ripple. Indeed that is a characteristic of all the Robichaux wives. No doubt for a very good reason, Tom. You have had immense practice at it.

Robichaux: Putt, you are being too hard on me dating back to the yard. Of course you do have a point. Terrible thing. Just terrible, because these Quakers take things so hard. Gil and Francis are suffering. So I sympathized with Francis of course.

Thatcher: Did you? He must have enjoyed that, having been notorious in the financial community for refusing to discuss your divorces. And then he went into seclusion during your alienation of affection suit.

Thatcher grins and laughs, as Tom grumbles indignantly.

Robichaux: Now Putt, what's that got to do with it? It's not the same thing at all. It's alright for me. Things slide off my back. But these Quakers take things so damned hard.

Thatcher nods.

After all, there's no point in all this if you don't enjoy it.

Thatcher: I think you hit the nail on the head again, Tom. Just wish you did it it more often with your stock underwriting.

Robichaux: So do I. You know the problem Putt. Just not enough good stocks; wish there were.

Robichaux looks down; Thatcher laughs.

Thatcher: Well, that clears the air. What about Olivia? Is she an ex-ambulance driver too?

Robichaux: No, no. She's a damned fine woman. Not my cup of tea, you understand.

Thatcher: No woman over 30 has ever been. Except in college you tended to like them older, but less than 30 even then.

He chuckles; Tom is a bit miffed.

Robichaux: A bit of experience helped back then; now a bit of youth is the thing.

Thatcher looks with respect upon Tom's wide experience as Tom continues.

Olivia's not a woman you forget easily. Seems sensible and cheerful and all that. But still you've got the feeling there's more there than meets the eye. You know, she's thinking a lot she isn't saying, still waters run deep and all that sort of thing.

Thatcher listens with respect to this expert on women. Robichaux brooded silently. Finally he shook his shoulders impatiently.

They're a funny couple when you come to think of it. I don't know that I ever have thought of that before. Icebergs, both of them. Nine-tenths submerged. And the funny thing is, I don't really think they're a bit alike.

Thatcher nodded.

Thatcher muttering: I'll have to remember that.

### Scene 10: Int.-Olivia's Living Room-Day

Ken Nicolls (out loud): So Mr. Thatcher sent me up here to console Mr. Withers, protect him from the news, and try to get him to be quiet. Seems like a role reversal. This place is amazing; one thing to see all the money on paper; another to see it proclaimed by acres of expensive land and quantities of museum quality antiques.

Here I am trying to buy a little brownstone in Brooklyn Heights and not quite able to do so. Jane expecting. Well there it is. Thatcher had told me to go to Michigan Motors and shake a solemn stick at them. It seemed to have worked. But going to Shaftesbury, Connecticut today was something else.

Phone rings. Houseman gives it to Nicolls.

Thatcher V.O.: We don't have much influence at the *World-Telegram*. But, you may hope that the *World-Telegram* has not penetrated to Shaftesbury, and thank God for *the Times*. A hardy tradition of journalism which believes in rigorously eschewing the institutional whenever the personal is available has protected whatever feelings as a banker Withers might be presumed to possess. Headlined "Blonde Beauty Slain in Connecticut—Café Society Triangle Unbared," the article dealt exclusively with the three principals. Peggy Lindsay emerged as a kind of fatal Lorelei luring Gilbert Austin onto the rocks of marital shipwreck; Gilbert Austin as a sybaritic pursuer of obscure and sinister pleasures of the flesh; and Olivia Austin as protector of hearth and home between her excursions into café society. But that's in the tabloids Nicholls, which Brad doesn't read. Unfortunately the press is in love with the antlers and they appear everywhere.

Nicolls: Sir, as you said, we can only wish this blows over.

They both nodded agreement over the phone. Withers walks in. Ken chooses to just hang up; Thatcher understands.

Withers: Nicolls, I don't know when I'll get down to the bank.

As he accepts documents Nicolls hands him.

Withers: Parker wants me around, and I feel I ought to stay. Mrs. Austin, my sister Olivia, you know, can't be abandoned.

Nicolls: Certainly, Sir.

Withers: God knows what's going on at the Sloan. I'll probably find that things there are a mess too.

There is a hint of hopefulness in his voice. Nicolls maintains respectful silence.

Withers: I particularly wanted to be there for the opening of the new employees' recreation room.

Nicolls: Is there anything I can do?

Withers hitched himself forward.

Withers: Don't know how long I'll have to stay here in Shaftesbury. John is just going to have to get along for a little while. Apart from the personal element, I have a feeling of . . . almost loyalty, you might say. Frankly, I gather that the police are in the dark, and I think the thing to do is to be very cooperative. Won't do to show them up, eh?

Nicolls: Oh no, sir.

Withers: What I thought you'd say. The difficulty is that that girl was killed any time from 4:30 PM on. Parker was out here yesterday. Told me the results of the medical stuff, you know. And they know she went into the village. So you see what that means. Somebody just left the parade and went inside, hit her on the temple. Oh, John did tell you about the Founders Day Parade, didn't he?

Nicolls: Er . . . yes.

Withers: Well, there you are. There's a good deal of confusion about where people were. Frankly, I think it's beyond the police. But one wants to put on a good show, under the circumstances. Although why anybody should want to kill that girl when she was clutching my antlers.

Nicolls: Clutching your antlers, sir?

Withers: That's what they seem to think. Either she was holding them, and I ask you, why should she? Or she was put on top of them. It's a shocking thing. You know, they tore her clothes.

Nicolls: Good heavens!

Withers: Yes, and there were some scratches on the body, too. Nothing dangerous—but grotesque, don't you know. Well, of course it makes you wonder.

Nicolls: It does.

Withers: They've impounded the antlers, as well. You know Nicolls, I wouldn't be a bit surprised if that fellow Parker hadn't exceeded his authority there. Hadn't thought of it before . . . but, you know, I may call up Carruthers and ask him for his opinion. It's one thing to be cooperative . . . but one can't have them taking liberties.

Nicolls: No, no.

Withers: I've told Olivia that she must answer any questions they ask. No need getting impatient when they keep coming out. We simply have to be courteous.

Nicolls: It will probably blow over..

Withers: I hope you're right. Well, let's get down to work. I was sorry to see that Hauser hadn't been able to keep this thing out of the papers. Knew I could rely on you. You're staying at the Inn? Good, you'll like it. They'll make you comfortable. And you're a lucky chap, let me tell you.

Nods to Nicolls in a warm way and leaves. Nicolls calls Thatcher to report in.

Nicolls: Everything fine so far. He left and may wander around.

Thatcher chuckles.

Thatcher (V.O.): Nicolls, he always wanders around, usually to far off places. Just keep him in town. Now as to the second step, tell Mr. and Mrs. Austin that now is no time for us to be digging around in their financial records. I think that both of them will realize it. I rather expect that there's no particular hurry about the divorce. And if they don't think so, I'm sure we can trust Carruthers to make it clear to them. And, Nicolls, there's no need for you to mention this point to Withers. Not only will it not have occurred to him, he will find it worthy of comment.

Nicolls: Yes, sir..

Thatcher V.O.: I trust, Nicolls, that I do not have to add that I rely upon you to do your best to keep Mr. Withers' comments centered firmly on noncontroversial areas. Talk about balancing the budget or unions if nothing else occurs to you. Miss Corsa called around to get people to come to see you at Olivia's. Gives you status, you know.

Nicolls: Yes, I understand sir.

Roger Kincaid and Bud walk in a few minutes later.

Roger Kincaid: Thatcher asked us to stop by. Saw Olivia a few minutes ago. She said she was going into the village. Did you know where she was going, Bud? Oh, this is Bud Austin, Mr. Nicolls.

Nicolls shook hands with the younger man.

Bud Austin: How do you do? No, I don't have any idea about Mother these days. Or Father either, since you insist that I be impartial about everything, Roger.

He sounded irritable.

Roger Kincaid: Are you here about the property settlement?

Nicolls: I have been detailed to offer aid and assistance to Bradford Withers, and to the Austins.

Bud Austin: We can thank God for that. At least we're going to be spared this insane divorce. I didn't understand it. And I'll bet that damn few people did. The Lord knows what Father thought he was doing.

Roger Kincaid: Bud, seeing that Peggy Lindsay has been murdered, that your mother and father, and the rest of us, have had the police in our hair ever since, don't you think you could refrain from adding coals to the fire?

Bud Austin: Well, it's so damn silly, at his age. And if you ask me, he wasn't very happy.

Roger Kincaid: If you ask me, if young Roger ever takes to criticizing me the way you're carping at your mother and father, I'll knock his block off even if he is 20 years old!

The tone was friendly, but it had its effect.

Bud Austin: It's been a shock, Roger.

Kincaid: I know.

Austin: You see, I've been kind of hoping . . . that is . . . now that Peggy isn't around . . . well, Mother and Father have always gotten along with each other.

Kincaid: Better change the subject, Bud. Did I tell you about the letter that young Roger sent us? He's going out for lacrosse.

They left together amicably. Nicolls calls in to report the goings on.

Nicolls: Mr. Thatcher, just saw Roger and Bud. They left amicably.

Thatcher V.O.: That young ass. Brad plans to inflict him on the Sloan. Now Nicolls, keep your eyes open. There's a lot in that situation up there that's interesting.

Nicolls leaves for the Inn.

## Scene 11: Int.-Bar & Restaurant-Day

**Nicolls enters.**

Madame Dumont: Mr. Nicolls, let me get you a hot toddy. Sit down and enjoy the fire.

Ken grIns and soon did so. Just then Mrs. Austin walks in, nods at Ken, and Madame Dumont starts talking to Mrs. Austin at the bar.

Madame Dumont: With such short notice it will be difficult for me. Very difficult, to do this new party.

Olivia Austin: I'm so sorry but I don't see that there's any choice.

Madame Dumont: Except to go on as we had planned.

Olivia Austin: That's out of the question.

Madame Dumont: It is not at all clear to me why that should be so. Everything has been arranged. The exhibitors, they are to stay here. But on the afternoon before the grand banquet, it was agreed that you would provide a cocktail party and kennel tour. Now you say no. But how then am I to prepare the *salle à manger?*

64

Olivia Austin: I cannot possibly be expected to entertain 65 people at a time like this.

Madame Dumont: It is the same time for all of us. My staff is greatly disturbed. But still I am preparing to receive 65 guests. And 70 dogs. It is not my habit to permit pets. For the sake of Shaftesbury I make an exception.

Olivia Austin: At a price.

Retorts Olivia nastily. Giselle is unmoved.

Madame Dumont: This is a public institution. Naturally I charge for the use of its facilities.

Olivia Austin: Oh, for heaven's sake, Giselle, stop pretending you don't understand. First, I'm left by my husband, and now I've got a murder to cope with. I'll be damned if I'm going to play the gracious hostess on top of it all.

Madame Dumont: Now that it's useful, you bring your husband into it. But it's only since the poor Peggy's death that you are upset. It's the vulgar publicity you dislike. When Gilbert left you, were you being upset then? No! You are too proud. It is all calmness and composure. Then you were perfectly willing to play the hostess! You insist on it. Everything must go on as usual. You have nothing to be ashamed of. Let the others back down, but not you. For a woman of heart, *then* was the time to be upset with poor Gilbert needing your help. You should have gone to him and . . .

Olivia Austin: You leave 'poor Gilbert' out of this!

Madame Dumont: You want to bring your husband in or leave him out, just as is convenient for you. If we are to talk about people being upset by Peggy's death, it is Gilbert who is upset. It is a breakdown one should fear for him. And he is my guest when you come suddenly asking me to give large cocktail parties.

Olivia Austin: It's a public institution, remember?

Madame Dumont: For Gilbert, it is a home in his hour of need.

Olivia Austin: He's not your guest, he's your client!

The double entendre struck home.

Madame Dumont: So, you insult me in my own Inn!

Olivia Austin: I'll insult you anytime and anywhere you have the impertinence to lecture me on my marriage!

Madame Dumont's reply was lost forever to Ken. A hand fell on his shoulder.

Donald Lindsay: Say, do you know what's going on over there? Well, it looks like the lady of the manor has come down off the pedestal. Good for you, Giselle, pitch it on hot and heavy.

Madame Dumont was appalled at this unexpected support.

Madame Dumont: Donald, be a good boy and go away. This is not for you. Mrs. Austin and I are discussing a cocktail party.

Donald Lindsay: A cocktail party, is it? That isn't the way it sounded from where I was standing. Why so shy, Giselle? Go on and give her hell. You were doing fine.

Olivia regains her full poise as Giselle starts tangling with Donald.

Madame Dumont: It is your imagination, Donald. There is nothing at all. It is only that Mrs. Austin does not find it convenient to give a party during the dog show.

Donald Lindsay: Oh, Mrs. Austin doesn't find it convenient, does she? And of course we all have to be very careful about what's convenient for Mrs. Austin.

Olivia Austin: You've been drinking.

Donald Lindsay: And what if I have? Does no one have the right to grieve as long as the Austins keep a stiff upper lip? Oh, it's easy enough for you. What have you got to be sorry for? Everything's lovely in your garden now. Just a decent moment of silence and then we can all go on as if nothing ever happened. The perfect couple with the perfect family. Tell me, does it ever cross the still surface of that immobile mind of yours that my sister would be alive today if she hadn't gotten mixed up with your pretty little lot? Or are you so bloody thankful to have your problem neatly removed by the mortuary truck that you can't think of anything else?

Madame Dumont: Stop this at once. You do not realize what you're doing.

Donald Lindsay: You! You're just as bad as she is. You're not weeping in your beer for poor Peggy. Oh, no! You're too busy trying to fill her shoes. It's *cher Gilbert* this and poor little Gilbert that. Must have peace and quiet for good old Gil. Afraid to quarrel with his wife while you play the ministering angel to him in his troubles. What's so special about his troubles? What's he done to deserve all this sympathy? Hell, if he weren't Gil Austin it isn't sympathy he'd be getting. Plenty of guys have murdered in his place. All he's done.

Madame Dumont: Donald!

Olivia Austin: No, Giselle. Let him go on.

Donald Lindsay: That's right. Always the perfect lady willing to listen to the tenants. Well, let me tell you, you may be able to hush up everyone else but you damned well can't keep me quiet. What do I care about your precious reputation? Who the hell do you Austins think you are anyway? Gil comes romping down from Ridge Road to play around with Peggy. She was too good for him if you want the truth. He finally gets her in trouble and you don't see why that should make . . .

Olivia Austin: Are you trying to tell me that Gil got Peggy pregnant? That she was going to have his child? Answer me, you contemptible little worm!

Donald Lindsay: Very good. A fine performance of shocked realization. As if you didn't know all along.

Olivia advanced, stiff-legged, in his direction. Her voice was menacingly hoarse as she swept aside his interruption.

Olivia Austin: So! Peggy was pregnant and you were all playing it for everything you could get! Oh, how blind can one be! A chance to recoup the family fortunes. What a godsend for the likes of you.

Donald Lindsay: Now look here, that's my sister you're talking about.

Olivia Austin: You! A picture of fraternal grief. Why, you've been living on Peggy since the day you put on long pants! You've never worked a day in your life. Look at you, drinking yourself into a stupor because you thought you were in a featherbed for life. Talk about sheer stupidity! This takes a prize of some sort. And what role in all this did the devoted brother play? Were you the go-between? I believe that's common practice in some circles.

Donald Lindsay: You can't say that to me.

Olivia Austin: 25 years of marriage down the drain because of a barnyard mistake. It's hilarious. How much you all must have enjoyed it. Gil Austin, passionate lover.

There came an interruption. What was that?

Gilbert Austin: Er, did you want me?

Olivia Austin: Join us by all means. We're just discussing your paternal feats. You didn't tell me you were expecting to become a father.

Gilbert Austin: Oh, lord. Olivia, if you'll just give me a chance to explain.

Olivia Austin: Don't you say another word to me. When I think what I've gone through for you! When I remember what I've done to try and keep my family together! And Peggy Lindsay tried to make me fight for you! For you! I could laugh now. You've made a fool of me, yourself, and of her.

Gilbert Austin: Olivia, you've got to listen to me. You mustn't say these things.

Olivia Austin: I won't listen to you! I'll say anything I please. It's time somebody did. When I think how she looked, coming to me all fury, talking about the house, ranting about you, and complaining about the three of us going to dinner together that night. What an idiot I was not to see the nose in front of my face. All the time you were . . .

Donald Lindsay: I knew it. I knew she wasn't going to see Withers that afternoon. But I thought she was trotting off to Gil somehow. But all the time it was you!

Gilbert Austin: You shut up, Lindsay! I know it wasn't that way, Livvy. You're just upset . . .

Olivia Austin: Don't you dare touch me! You unspeakable . . . What do I care? Of course it's true. I should have known from the beginning. And it was all wasted, wasted. Leave me alone, all of you. I can't stand any more. If you try and stop me, I'll scream.

Olivia rushes by her husband out the door.

### Scene 12: Int-Bar & Restaurant-Day

Ken Nicolls out loud quietly: Why did I let Uncle George persuade me to go into banking.

Donald Lindsay out loud: Better leave; what a mess.

Ken falls back into his chair. Lindsay can't get under way.

Madame Dumont: Gilbert, come sit down. You must not let this distress you more.

Gilbert Austin remains immobile, clearly at the end of his tether. The flinging open of the front door released him. Roger Kincaid burst in, breaking the immobility.

Roger Kincaid: What's going on here? I saw Olivia tearing out of here. What is it? By God, Donald have you caused more trouble?

Austin recovers.

Gilbert Austin: Nothing. There's no trouble, Roger. We've just had a misunderstanding.

Donald Lindsay: Misunderstanding!

This roused Madame Dumont.

Madame Dumont: Donald, get out. Now! I don't want you here. Out!

Since it was clear that Roger Kincaid, if not Gilbert Austin, would be happy to lend force to Madame Dumont's injunction, Donald Lindsay had no alternative. He leaves.

Madame Dumont: Good. It is good that you are here, Roger. You can join us in a drink, which we all need. And perhaps you too, Mr. Nicolls.

With drink in hand Austin speaks to Roger.

Gilbert Austin: Olivia found out, Roger. Now, there's nothing I can do!

### Scene 13: Int.-Olivia's Living Room-Day

Olivia walks into her living room.

Olivia Austin outloud: Well that's that. Glad I burned off some of it. Now back to myself. Yes, I regret the outburst but that's the end of that.

She sits down and calms herself. Then Brad walks in.

Withers: Just came over to see you and escape all the goings on.

Olivia Austin: Fine. Ring for Althea and get her to make your drink and bring me a sherry.

He does; he returns; Olivia sits opposite Brad and leans back.

Withers: You're looking a little tired, Liv. You've been wonderfully strong but Carrie says, she wrote today, by the way, that you want to keep up your strength.

Olivia Austin: Yes.

Althea brings a tray of drinks into the living room, sets it between them, and withdraws.

Withers: Now Olivia, there are a few things that I want to talk to you about.

Olivia Austin: Maybe you'd better hear my news first.

She tells him.

Withers: Who would have thought it of Gil? Of all people! Carrie is never going to believe this.

71

Olivia Austin: Brad!

Withers: Can't help feeling sorry for him, once you understand. Terrible thing.

Olivia Austin: I do not feel sorry for Gil.

Withers: Still, it explains a lot. Why he did it, I mean. Being a Quaker and all.

Olivia Austin: Did what? God knows Gil is the greatest fool it has been my misfortune to encounter! But I can assure you of one thing—he didn't kill Peggy Lindsay!

She laughs, Brad looks scared, and she storms out of the room. Alone in the living room, Bradford Withers is suddenly deeply troubled.

### Scene 14: Int.-Bar and Restaurant-Day

Nicolls: Sir they just left the bar. It was a heavyweight fight to end them all. Madame Dumont and Mrs. Austin were the main event; they each took down Donald with a single blow; Mrs. Austin found out Mr. Austin had gotten Peggy Lindsay pregnant, that sent Mrs. Austin into even better fighting form and she demolished Donald Lindsay as a leach, Mrs. Austin stormed out but with her brass and elegance probably is OK. Roger Kincaid stormed in and broke it up, called Lindsay to account, Madame Dumont tossed Lindsay. Sir, it was a brawl of a lifetime.

Thatcher V.O.: Sounds it; wished I had seen it; can't stand Lindsay; a pleasure to see him tossed; and Olivia at her peak is without equal though I'll bet Giselle gave her a good bout.

Nicolls warming to it all and growing up in the process.

Nicolls: She did, sir. Mrs. Austin won, but only on points. Madame Dumont went the distance. Roger was magnificent.

72

Thatcher V.O.: Don't let yourself get shaken by a scene. Try to see them tomorrow. And Nicolls, keep me informed.

Nicolls out loud: Seems I have made this place home.

The locals considered him a local with some envy for his expense account.

Fred (50, solid): I always said that still waters run deep, our Gilbert. Roger! You're the boy who can tell us the latest.

Kincaid: No, I don't know a thing, Fred.

Fred persisted.

Fred: About the pregnancy, I mean.

Kincaid: Let's just drop it. Nicolls join me.

Nicolls waved no and left the bar for his room. In the morning he returned to the bar & restaurant and saw Bud Austin who waved him over.

Bud Austin: I have to talk to Dad. That's why I'm here but he's already gone out. Probably couldn't face me. God knows how I'm going to break this terrible news to Nancy.

Nicolls: Nancy?

Bud Austin: My wife. She's . . . that is, we're expecting our first child. I'm up at the Business School, you know.

Nicolls: Why is it so many Harvard MBA students are married and have children before graduating?

Bud Austin is clearly out of his depth so moves on.

Bud Austin: I wouldn't say it to everybody, but I understand that you were here when Mom found out. About Peggy's pregnancy I mean.

Bud then blushes violently, then frowns. Nicolls nods as Bud plows on.

Everybody in Shaftesbury is talking about it, you know. I don't know how Dad could do a thing like this to me.

It was clear that getting Peggy Lindsay pregnant was in no way similar to the activity of himself and Nancy in producing a child.

And Mom is heartbroken. Disgusting. I'm going to do what I can to support Mom, of course.

Ken didn't think heartbroken was a good description but remains silent. Bud charges out, nodding importantly at Ken on the way by.

Nicholls mutters: With enough Bud Austins in the world, it should be possible to become a John Thatcher. In fact, it should be a cinch.

Just as Nicolls is about to leave finally, Donald Lindsay and Roger Kincaid come in to have some coffee it would seem. Nicolls quietly retreats to a chair, thinking rightly Thatcher would want him to eavesdrop on the goings on.

Donald Lindsay: I thought you might understand.

They get coffees and two donuts and sit down at the bar.

Kincaid: Look, Don. I'm sorry as hell about this story about Peggy, but what good is it going to do you or your mother if you go around telling . . .

Lindsay: Story! What do you mean, story? Ask the coroner! She was carrying his child. Your holier-than-thou Gil Austin.

Kincaid: All right. I believe you. We all do. The whole town believes you, Don, and we're sorry. But what good is it doing anybody to stir up all of this dirt?

Lindsay: I'll tell you. It's going to cost someone plenty, that's what good it will do! Hell, Roger, thought you might be more human than the Austins because you're as poor as we are, but I guess that just working for them makes you sure that they can get away with murder.

Kincaid: Shut up, Don, You're upset . . . or maybe drunk.

Lindsay: Very funny, Roger! Very funny, especially from you. Well, look who's here. Enjoying your stay in picturesque old Shaftesbury, are you, Mr. Nicolls? Sorry I can't stay to talk to you but I've got a lot of people to see. Bye Roger. Be seeing you.

They watched him stagger out of the bar.

Kincaid: You wouldn't believe it, but normally we get along very well in Shaftesbury. Quiet, and all that sort of thing.

Nicolls: I don't suppose you can blame people for being on edge. Murder changes things.

Kincaid: I guess so. I would have sworn that you'd never see Shaftesbury seething with gossip the way it is. But I guess you're right. Murder changes things. Bud around? His father's up at the farm, so I'm picking him up while I'm down here.

Nicolls: He left here a few minutes ago to walk up there I think.

Roger and Ken both get up to leave.

### Scene 15: Int.-New York Bar & Restaurant-Day

Thatcher: Good to get away from Brad's calls. Glad you could join me. Seven urgent phone calls from Brad has almost reduced me to silly putty. I have to call Miss Corsa, before we have our coffee.

Robichaux and Trinkam chortled.

You've made a note of that, haven't you, Miss Corsa.

Miss Corsa V.O: A note of what, Mr. Thatcher?

Thatcher: Of what Mr. Withers wants.

She pauses and then said says,

Miss Corsa (V.O.): Mr. Withers did not want anything. He just wanted to talk.

Thatcher: Oh.

Trinkam: Game to Rose, again.

Robichaux: Francis has known for days. Austin told him about the girl's pregnancy right after the murder. Haven't seen hide or hair of him since. Hard on these Quakers. Helluva thing for a Quaker. That's the trouble. No experience.

Charlie nodded. Both of them nodded their heads in sober deprecation.

Thatcher: You both have superior positions. Tom, harrumphing his way through life amidst a series of deeply felt grievances directed toward taxation, high salaries, and government supervision, cherishes an ineradicable fondness for marriage with young women. Charlie, on the other hand, has avoided marriage with a dexterity and *brio* buttressed by continual increments to her experience with rich, ripe, and seasoned men. You even survived your brief engagement to a young Greek God contracted in a moment's aberrant attraction toward the pleasures of domesticity.

Robichaux: Putt, you just don't understand his kind. You either, Charlie. And I can't say that I blame you. He just didn't know what was the right thing to do.

Trinkam: You're joking.

Robichaux: No, you don't know these good men. It can be really hard to live with, let me tell you. Francis accepts me, sinner though I am in his mind. That's hard for him.

Thatcher: To expand this, what about good women?

Robichaux: John, you know I don't know any and never did, not to be with that is. But they have a lot more sense than their male counterparts. Take Olivia Austin, Carrie Withers, or your dear departed wife, John. They know what men are good for and what they aren't, and never expect too much from them. Smart policy.

Thatcher: You are right. I was thinking of Olivia Austin.

Robichaux: She is a remarkable woman and you could count on her to display more balanced judgment than her husband or almost anyone else for that matter. And her brother, your revered President, too.

Trinkam: That would not be difficult.

Thatcher: My latest bulletins from the front indicate that balanced judgment was a missing attribute Olivia Austin displayed upon being informed of her husband's situation.

Robichaux was on sure ground when it came to women. Waving aside Olivia's outburst.

Robichaux: The heat of the moment. She got her balance after leaving I expect.

Thatcher: Exactly what she did Tom.

Robichaux: Putt, thanks for not piling on about my confession. I wish I did it more. I admire her for doing so. Admirable woman.. Too much for me of course.

They nodded together.

Trinkam: Can you blame her? All this mess because of a little slip-up. She probably doesn't like being made a fool of.

Robichaux shook his head sadly.

Robichaux: They never do.

Thatcher: Must be something else. She must be worried Gil might have killed Peggy.

Robichaux: Look, Charlie, you two want to think of the future. There's this little drug firm in Mexico that's come up with something really new. They say they've got a pill that combines diet control and contraception. It will make a mint.

Thatcher: I wish you two were as good at picking stocks as you are understanding women.

Trinkam: In my case men.

They all chuckled over more coffee.

Thatcher: You know, I think Olivia is capable of anything. Of course she could be acting. But if not, then she was in the grip of some truly overpowering emotion. And in that case, I would like to know what it was.

Robichaux and Trinkam sat in silence.

Robichaux: Well that's the kind of thing you are expert at, John.

## Chapter 16: Int.-Olivia's Living Room-Day

Nicolls out loud. Here I am on schedule at 10:30 AM per my phone appointment. To offer this experienced lady, gracious hostess, and well known Clubwoman, advice about money when she has a thousand times more than I have and the family has for over 150 years. Rather absurd, but a lot has seemed that way since I came up here.

He knocks on the door. Althea answers.

Althea (Attractive woman of 25): Mrs. Austin isn't home and she doesn't have any statements to make anyway.

Nicolls: You might remember me from yesterday. I'm not a reporter. And I have an appointment with Mrs. Austin. My name is Nicolls.

She saw what looked like a young Greek God when she peeked out at him.

Althea: Oh yes, Mr. Nicolls. I remember you from yesterday. There have been so many people pestering us, I didn't even look out the door. Mrs. Austin is over at the kennel, Mr. Nicolls. I will go over and get her. Make yourself at home. Can I get you some coffee?

Nicolls: How nice of you. It is a big strain isn't it?

Althea smiles at the human Mr. Nicolls and clearly indicates she wished more people like him showed up.

Athea: Yes, sir.

A few minutes later Mrs. Austin arrives.

Olivia Austin: Mr. Nicolls, I thought that I would get back to the house in time. Althea was quite taken with you; she liked the way you handled Brad. I'll be sure to tell John.

Olivia knew how to spread the butter and make a new ally.

Nicolls: So nice of you, Mrs. Austin.

Olivia Austin: Will take some of the sting out of it for the various goings on you have suffered of late.

Nicolls: Thank you again.

Olivia had made another conquest. Roger Kincaid appeared at the door behind her.

Roger Kincaid: Hello, Nicolls. Listen, Olivia, don't worry. Whatever it is, we'll get it cleared up before the show.

Olivia Austin: I hope so. It's Bold Baron. He's been sick.

Ken nodded politely trying to conceal his fear of these Dobermans he had seen snarling at him behind the kennel fence when walking up from the Inn.

Nicolls: Sorry to hear that, with your Show coming up.

Roger Kincaid: See you later Olivia; bye Nicolls.

Olivia Austin: Roger is a pillar of strength, but I know that he's worried. And if anything happens to Bold Baron we'll really be in the soup.

Donald Lindsay knocks on the door. Nicolls notices Olivia is tired. Althea has not come back.

Nicolls: I'll get it.

Donald Lindsay: I want to talk to her.

Pushes Nicolls aside and walks in.

Olivia Austin: Donald, I have nothing to say to you.

Ken wondered uneasily if he would be required to knock the man down.

Donald Lindsay: You may have nothing to say to me, but I have something to say to you.

Olivia: Don't be more of a fool than God made you, Donald. I'm sorry about Peggy. Truly I am. But I'm not going to put up with you.

Lindsay noticed Ken squaring off. Weakly,

Donald Lindsay: Stop that Nicolls.

Olivia Austin: Donald, in two minutes I'll let Nicolls knock you down, throw you out, and call the police. I want you to get out of here. Now.

Lindsay wavered. Then with a look both furtive and menacing, he left. They just looked at each other for a few moments. Olivia spoke first.

How exceptionally disagreeable.

Nicolls: Yes.

Althea brought their drinks. They sipped them for awhile. Nicolls is surprised she remembered his drink, as she smiles at him. Olivia sees through her and chuckles. Nicolls just drinks.

Withers opens the door.

Withers: Liv! Liv! Want to talk to you a minute!

Olivia Austin mutters: Oh dear.

Withers: Hello there, Nicolls!

Olivia Austin: We're having a business conference, Brad. What is it you wanted?

Withers: Just wanted to warn you about that damned sod, Donald Lindsay!

Olivia Austin: Yes, we've . . .

Withers: Pushed his way into my place just now! Muttering a lot of things—didn't understand a word he was ranting, Liv, but he sounded ugly. I threw him out, but I want to warn you not to talk to him. Roger says he's spreading a lot of talk around town, you know.

Olivia Austin: Yes, Brad.

Withers: The man's likely to be a nuisance. You say that you two are talking business? I think that I may join you for coffee.

Ken sympathizes with his hostess.

Olivia Austin: We are ahead of you, Brad. We are drinking which you can see. We need it.

Althea: Mrs. Austin. There's a telephone call for you.

She takes it and then says.

Olivia Austin: The police. Captain Parker is on his way up here. It was courteous of him to call, don't you think?

Withers: Not again! They've been in and out of here for days. Well, Liv, we'll stand by.

Chief knocks on the door. Althea is back to answer. Althea ushers him in.

Parker: Mrs. Austin, I hear you had a fight with Donald Lindsay at the Inn yesterday. He told me that you admitted seeing Peggy Lindsay last Sunday. Why didn't you tell us that?

Olivia Austin: I don't like your tone, Captain.

Parker: Mrs. Austin, Peggy Lindsay was murdered. My tone doesn't matter. Did you or did you not fight with her?

Olivia Austin: I suppose that there's no use denying it since everybody in Shaftesbury knows that I did.

Withers: Don't admit anything. Not a word until we get hold of Carruthers.

      Olivia ignores him.

Olivia Austin: Peggy Lindsay and I had an exchange of words..

Parker: What about?

Olivia Austin: We argued about Ridge Road Farm, if you must know. Not content with stealing my husband, she was accusing me of all sorts of things simply because she wanted my home. It was extremely vulgar. I lost my temper and that's all.

Parker: Not about the pregnancy? They're saying in town that you learned about the baby and lost your temper.

Olivia Austin: Not about the pregnancy. She wanted the farm and I wanted it. That's all.

      Remembered distaste curled her lips.

Parker: What time was this?

Olivia Austin: About four o'clock. She stormed in, blew up with accusations, then stormed out, really before I had a chance to say anything.

Parker: You mean that's the way you learned that your husband . . .

Olivia Lindsay: I had not learned about Peggy Lindsay's pregnancy until that wretched Donald Lindsay . . .

Withers: Olivia!

Parker: Mrs. Austin, I would like to talk to you in private.

Olivia Austin: Certainly. Brad, Mr. Nicolls, perhaps you can take a walk.

They leave. A few minutes later Parker comes out. Nicolls and Withers go back in.

Olivia Austin: I'm going upstairs Brad. I will see you tomorrow.

Brad takes this meekly and leaves.

Mr. Nicolls. Feel free to stay here; Althea evidently likes you and will enjoy making a wonderful dinner for you as well as supplying you with drink. Good night.

She leaves. Nicolls has that drink that Althea brings in and settles down to relax a bit before calling Thatcher.

Thatcher V.O.: She said what?

Nicolls: That's what she said, Mr. Thatcher.

Thatcher V.O.: Good Lord, Nicolls, couldn't you or Withers stop her? That farm is a drop in the bucket in their estate and Parker knows it. Why should she and Peggy fight about that, when she gets into murderous rages just hearing about the pregnancy . . . ?

Nicolls: I really don't know, sir. I just wanted to tell you about this. And ask if I should stay.

Thatcher V.O.: Obviously.

Nicolls: And to tell you that you will no doubt be hearing from Withers.

Thatcher V.O.: If you're being sarcastic, stop it. Were they going to arrest Mrs. Austin?

Nicolls: I don't think so, sir. But the police were certainly not very friendly.

Thatcher V.O.: Fine.

He glares at the phone as if to dare it to ring again. It does.

Miss Corsa V.O.: Mr. Withers.

Withers calling from Olivia's Living Room; Nicolls has stepped out.

Withers: John! John, things are terrible up here. The police are after Olivia . . .

Thatcher V.O.: Now Brad . . .

Withers: She admits having a fight with Peggy Lindsay. It's all over town anyway. Says that the girl marched in at about four o'clock, started abusing her, then just raced off in the middle of things . . .

Thatcher V.O.: Nicolls told me . . .

Withers: . . . of course Peggy was alive after that but it doesn't look good, does it? John, do you suppose that you could come up . . . ?

They hang up.

Thatcher V.O. out loud: Nicolls is revenged.

### Scene 17: Int.-Thatcher's Office-Day

85

Thatcher: Miss Corsa, I see you eying the pile of papers I haven't done anything about. Well you are right. You usually are.

Miss Corsa does not approve of Thatcher's friviolity and shows it.

Well now I have to gather the gang, as it should be called, or team, more professionally but less accurately. But first we have to gather our gang and plan the attack on Shaftesbury, Connecticut.

He grins; she taps her pen on her dictation book.

But I think it is excessive for us to attend the funeral. We will leave it to Nicolls. It will be good for him.

Miss Corsa lifts an eyebrow.

Alright. It won't be good for him but it will save the rest of us.

Phone rings.

Miss Corsa: Mr. Withers.

Withers V. O.: It would mean a lot to Olivia if you came up for the funeral.

Thatcher: Brad, let me speak to Olivia.

Withers V.O.: Well, she has actually gone.

Thatcher: Bye Brad.

Hangs up. Another call.

Miss Corsa: Mr. Carruthers.

With more unintended respect in her voice.

Carruthers V.O.: John, it could be worse. Your young man, Nicolls, can tell you about it. The quarrel with the Lindsay girl doesn't look good, but at least she was seen on her way back to the village after she left Mrs. Austin. With all this the police have to be careful, you know. So long as there's no evidence of a fight down at the Inn, Mrs. Austin should be alright. Of course, that's just my opinion. I'm not a criminal attorney, you know. I just handle the estate.

Thatcher: Yes, but as you know it is your chief function as the Withers' legal adviser at the moment to remind the police of "all this." No one has more experience than you in conveying such information with a maximum of delicacy and a minimum of ambiguity.

They both chuckled. Miss Corsa and Thatcher get a good deal of work done.

Miss Corsa: Mr. Withers on the line.

Withers V.O.: John, just as well you didn't come. Terrible. Young Lindsay was a disgrace; everyone was curious; Olivia was magnificent; Gilbert was tougher than people realize. Those Quakers are tough like Devane. Roger was the best of them; went off fixing a barb wire fence. Left the house afterwards to give Olivia some peace. Managed to get them all through it. Wonder what's next.

Thatcher: Well done Brad. Now back to the bank work here.

Withers V.O.: Bank work; the dog show is opening. Have to pay attention to that. Now you can come up safely and help us through it.

Brad hangs up and buzzes Miss Corsa.

Thatcher: Get the plane; going back to Shaftesbury. By the time we are through the pilot will know it all too well, as will I.

## Scene 18: Int.-Olivia's Living Room-Day

Olivia Austin: Thank you for coming back, John. Brad was at his best with the family at the funeral. It was good to see; the rest were quite terrible.

Thatcher: As you expected.

    Olivia smiles elegantly.

Now this Dog Show. Olivia, I beg to be released from all of that.

Olivia Austin: We will have you do the same thing again with Roger getting your place card again.

    As her eyes twinkled.

You will come down to the bar as a show of force; I will get your place setting tag for the big dinner; and you can eat and drink safely in the bar.

Thatcher: Thank you Olivia. I do think I have the pieces to this puzzle; I just haven't been able to fit them together yet.

Olivia Austin: You will, John. You will. The Dog Show comes at a good time. Gives everyone something to do. Gilbert wants to see you. I said he could in 30 minutes. So I'll be off.

    She leaves. Gilbert Austin knocks 30 minutes later and comes in.

Gilbert Austin: You look comfortable, Thatcher. Good someone is.

    Smiles engagingly.

Wanted to tell you Lindsay has been calling me. Something about money and Ridge Road Farm. Brad blew up of course. Donald said he wanted to see me.

88

Thatcher speaks gently.

Thatcher: Gil, why are you telling me this? What made you think it was important? That may help.

Austin: John, Brad was outraged and said, "That little runt hasn't give up yet. He still thinks he's going to make his fortune out of you." But I don't think Donald's was trying to capitalize in this instance on the fact that he almost became my brother-in-law. Something was different in his tone. He said he had some information I might be interested in.

Thatcher: What did you say to that?

Austin: Told him I was too busy to speak with him tonight. Considering the way he blew up at Bud this afternoon, I could scarcely sit down with him at the Inn for a cozy chat.

Withers knocks and comes in.

Withers: John, Mrs. Lindsay was putting an act on all day, collapsing this afternoon, but she was well enough this morning to see Peggy's insurance agent!

Thatcher and Austin both stared as Withers produced this tidbit.

Thatcher: Where did you hear about that?

Withers: Er . . . as a matter of fact, Giselle happened to mention it this afternoon. Just dropped down to see her after Olivia and Bud left.

Under the accusing stares, Withers' voice became mildly defiant.

Not what you think at all. Just wanted to straighten out this business about the antlers, that's all.

Thatcher says with rising exasperation.

Thatcher: Brad, what business about the antlers?

Withers: Some damn nonsense the police have dreamed up. They want to keep the antlers. I just wanted to assure Giselle, Madame Dumont, that I would leave no stone unturned . . . that is. . .

Faced with Withers' rapid degeneration into complete incoherence, Thatcher abandons the antlers and returns to a subject which interested him more.

Thatcher: About this insurance on Peggy. What was her coverage?

Withers: Giselle didn't know.

Thatcher: You surprise me.

Withers leaves. Nicolls arrives.

Thatcher: Brad mentioned Peggy's insurance, which he heard about from Madame Dumont.

They share a knowing glance.

It's surprising nobody's mentioned this insurance before. Of course its value could be nominal in view of Peggy Lindsay's expectations.

Nicolls. You are right, sir. Oh, a girl like that wouldn't be apt to carry much.

Thatcher says tartly.

Thatcher: That girl was making over $75,000 per year.

Nicolls: From dogs?

Thatcher: Yes. You will learn, Nicolls, that specialists make money. They are some of our best, steadiest, and richest clients.

So I know it seems odd now, but she was one of the best known dog handlers in New England and that means money. Big money.

Nicolls: But, good Lord, sir, if she'd been a man making a salary like that with a wife and children . . .

Thatcher: Exactly. A coverage of two hundred thousand dollars would not be unusual in her position. But in her position would she be likely to go in for that much?

Nicolls recovers.

Nicolls: That mother of hers would have seen to it.

Thatcher: Excellent, Nicolls. I was thinking the same thing.

Nicolls: If she was making that much money, why do the Lindsays run around Shaftesbury acting as if they were sharecroppers? Donald made some remark the other day about the Lindsays and the Kincaids being poor.

Thatcher, impressed by Nicolls recovering and getting it, responds kindly.

Thatcher: Because in Shaftesbury people don't think much in terms of earned income. It's capital they think about there. You don't run around raising beef cattle at a spectacular loss if you're operating on a salary. It's a different kind of money altogether. And not one you see much of these days outside of communities like Shaftesbury. But, I might remind you, one of the other places you see it is at the Sloan.

Ken sank into an abashed silence which Thatcher did not disturb. Then continues,

It's not hard to see how Olivia Austin and Peggy Lindsay wouldn't see eye to eye on Ridge Road Farm, but it's not much

91

of a story to explain their last quarrel. How exactly did Mrs. Austin put it?

Nicolls: She was pretty crisp with Parker about the whole thing. Just said Peggy Lindsay had come up and made a vulgar attempt to steal the house. But after Parker left, Mr. Withers insisted on going over the whole thing again.

Thatcher: Naturally. Did she divulge any additional detail in the second round?

Nicolls: In a way. She said Peggy started the whole thing off on the wrong foot by sticking her chin out and saying it was time they settled the thing like rational adults. She, Peggy, that is, wasn't going to have Gil taken advantage of.

Thatcher: Yes, Peggy Lindsay had no doubt nerved herself for the interview with Olivia and then, before her courage could fail her, had hurled herself into the subject with an abruptness and tactlessness guaranteed to render the entire interview fruitless. How the notable Mrs. Gilbert Austin must have felt, having mature rationality urged upon her by the chit who was stealing her husband and flaunting her proprietary rights!

It would be enough to make anyone lose his temper.

Nicolls: Mrs. Austin admits she lost hers, alright. Told Peggy what she thought of her behavior in no uncertain terms. Upstart, gold digger, all that sort of thing. Said she'd never let Peggy Lindsay queen it on Ridge Road. If she wanted to play lady of the manor she could have the decency to do it someplace else.

Thatcher: What then?

Nicolls: Then Peggy lost *her* temper. Called Mrs. Austin a thief. Said she was making hay out of Mr. Austin's easygoingness. According to Mrs. Austin she was just blazing with fury. But the thing that maddened Mrs. Austin the most was that after Peggy finished ripping her to shreds, saying every unforgivable thing in the book, she just came to a dead halt and slammed out of the house without waiting to hear the reply. Mrs. Austin said she had a pretty fiery denunciation all ready to be delivered.

Thatcher: And all of this quarrel revolved around the farm?

Nicolls: That's what Mrs. Austin told us. She went on to say that she was so upset, both from the quarrel and the frustration of being left in midstream, that it took her some time to get down to the parade. Once she was there she avoided people because she was still trying to calm herself down. She'd forgotten all about meeting her son.

Thatcher: The inference that everybody will draw, of course, is that she met Peggy again while she was still in a rage. Hmmm. Not a word about the pregnancy, I gather.

Nicolls: Not a word. Mrs. Austin insists she didn't know about that until Donald blew the lid off the whole thing.

Thatcher: It seems like a very one-track quarrel. If Peggy were that mad, you'd think she would have hurled her pregnancy into Olivia's teeth.

Nicolls: Mrs. Austin's fights do tend to cover a lot of ground.

Thatcher: She is reputed to be a lady of very equable temperament.

Nicolls: That may be her reputation, but in my book she seems fully capable of a murderous rage.

Thatcher: Well, you've been a witness to one. How long do you think it would last?

Nicolls: How long?

Thatcher: Yes. How long after the fight's over? Do you think she would still have been homicidal if she'd met Donald Lindsay an hour after their encounter the other day?

Nicolls: Oh, I see what you mean, sir. I just don't know.

Thatcher: After all, the important time is during the parade when everybody was milling around. You have no idea of the confusion that a parade can generate. People parking cars, refractory children being rounded up, bands playing, the entire staff of the Inn out front. And practically everybody who might have murdered Peggy Lindsay wandering about alone.

Nicolls: Didn't anybody see Peggy?

Thatcher: Nobody who'll admit to it. As a matter of fact, I'm almost sure Gilbert Austin met at least one of the Lindsays. I saw him that morning with Peggy and he was very pleased with himself. Oh, a little nervous about the dinner that night, but nothing more than social embarrassment. But when I met him later at the parade, he was fed up with the Lindsays. I wouldn't be surprised if he'd had a run-in with Donald Lindsay which he's keeping quiet. That's one of the reasons I'm worried about the boy's trying to get in touch with him now. If additional suspicion can be aimed at any Austin, Donald Lindsay will take real pleasure in doing it.

Nicolls nods.

We've only got his story about dropping Peggy at Mrs. Austin's that afternoon. He might have put her up to the whole thing and been waiting for her someplace where the Kincaids didn't see him. After all, Mrs. Kincaid said Peggy looked on her way to bawl somebody out. Maybe Donald let her in for more than she was prepared to take on.

But I am unprepared to believe that anybody in his right mind could have been persuaded into any action by Donald Lindsay.

94

There is no reason to suppose that Peggy had been mentally incompetent.

Nicolls: There's just one other thing while Mrs. Austin was telling us about her fight with Peggy, I got the impression maybe Mr. Withers might be holding something back. It was just an impression . . .

Thatcher: Of course he's holding something back. Anybody can see that. It's probably nothing more than some piece of nonsense with Madame Dumont that he doesn't want Carrie to find out about.

Nicolls: Carrie?

Thatcher: Mrs. Withers. Caroline Withers is a very forceful woman, a force of nature. When she gets home from the Bahamas, she'll find out what Withers was up to before the day's out. So I wouldn't waste time worrying about it. What I'd really like to know is what's going on between Gilbert and Olivia Austin.

Nicolls: How do you mean, sir?

Thatcher: They've both been behaving very strangely. Oh, I don't mean all this turmoil about Peggy's pregnancy. I mean their general aloofness toward each other. After all, they've been married for almost 25 years and Austin isn't a man to take his responsibilities lightly. But you don't find him rallying round in support. Of course, he may have tried and Olivia made it clear that his presence would be unwelcome. But still, it's very odd.

It could mean that they suspect each other. In fact, I wouldn't put it past either one of them to maintain a reticent silence in spite of being an eyewitness to the murder.

Withers bursts back in.

95

Withers: John, Lindsay was murdered last night. The body was found this morning by one of the farm hands in the Number Three field.

Thatcher: This means the the body was found on your place. We'll have to face things as they come. I suppose that we should thank God that the Black Angus is shorthorned.

Withers calmly pours a drink and one for John. Nicolls gets his own. He was growing up and looking it.

Thatcher finally leaves for home.

## Scene 19-Int.-Thatcher's Office-Day

Thatcher is finally back in New York and enters his office with a sigh. Gabler enters.

Gabler: This can't go on, John. I had to send the Strauss account off yesterday without your signature, and you know what that means!

Thatcher: Everett, Mrs. Strauss, 97, and a client for over 70 years. This will surely not be a problem. In Shaftesbury, you have a soulmate, Cynthia Kincaid, who thinks the worst and is often right as you are. I know there have been difficulties, but with Brad up in Shaftesbury . . .

Gabler pounces.

Gabler: That's another thing! Withers was supposed to be available for the Flinders contract. God knows why, but it's a good thing to have the President around when the bank undertakes large commitments . . . and Withers always enjoys it.

Thatcher: They've found another body. And it's on Withers' estate.

Gabler halts in mid-sentence.

Gabler: A body?

Thatcher: Another murder.

Gabler opened his mouth, shut it, takes off his rimless glasses, gave them a savage swipe, then, with some waspishness, resumed his discourse.

Gabler: I have not complained about the serious inconveniences caused to the Trust Department by Withers' frequent and unscheduled absences, whether for tuna fishing, grouse shooting or stalking whatever it is that he stalks.

Thatcher: Now Everett.

Gabler: We've adjusted to Withers but John, when he starts dragging you off for these, these entertainments, then I frankly find it difficult to see how we will be able to get any work done.

Miss Corsa buzzes.

Miss Corsa: Mr. Withers, Mr. Thatcher.

Thatcher: Put him through.

Thatcher swivels away from Everett Gabler's martially accusing eye. Gabler clearly regards murder as some sort of sporting activity.

How bad are things?

Withers V.O.: Terrible. Everybody up here is in a pretty bad state, too. There was some sort of protest meeting at the Grange this morning. Anyway, I want you to say a word to Hauser about the publicity.

Thatcher: I don't know how we're going to soft-pedal publicity when there are two murders to cope with. At least you're spared reporters swarming around.

Withers V.O.: Well, I should hope so. I'd like to know what we pay taxes for if we can't get cooperation from the village authorities.

Thatcher: What are the police doing?

Withers V.O.: The police? Well, they're all over the place of course. Asking the damnedest things about what we were doing when Lindsay got himself killed, in the middle of the night. Everybody was in bed or at least everybody says they were in bed. Dammit, John, you were here. Gil was back at the Inn. Olivia stayed home, Roger was in and out of the kennel with Bold Baron, and let me tell you, we've all had to put up with a good deal of impertinence from that man Parker. I'm beginning to get incensed about his attitude. They're nagging at Olivia . . .

Thatcher: I don't suppose you're going to be able to get down to the bank then. We need you here.

This patent falsehood consoles Withers.

Withers V.O.: Don't see that I can leave. I know that Gil wants to get back too, but they're keeping us here.

Thatcher yields to temptation.

Thatcher: And how is Mrs. Lindsay?

Withers V.O.: Pretty hysterical.

Thatcher: You might find out if Donald Lindsay carried a lot of insurance. Well, I'll keep in touch. Goodbye.

He hangs up abruptly. Trinkam walks in.

And that, Everett, is that.

Gabler leaves. Bowman calls through.

Bowman V.O.: You're back? Good! Now, John, you have to take a look at this trucking stock situation. I'll send the figures up. The market's picking them up. I've cleared this with Charlie and I want us to move fast. So, if you . . .

Thatcher moved the receiver an inch from his ear.

Thatcher: Hold it a minute, Walter. Yes, Miss Corsa?

Miss Corsa looked at her harassed chief from the doorway.

Miss Corsa: Miss Prettyman says that three Indian businessmen have an appointment with Mr. Withers at four this afternoon, because Mr. Withers told her he would be back today.

She sidesteps Thatcher's scowl and continues. Miss Prettyman is Miss Corsa's arch foe. Thatcher scowls at her but she stands her ground.

And should she cancel the appointment or do you want to see them?

Thatcher: I do not want to see them.

Miss Corsa, correctly interpreting this as irrelevant, waits for his considered opinion.

Why don't we do business with the Swiss? Alright. I'll take them. Four o'clock? You'd better tell Gabler that I won't be at his meeting. Walter—still there? You're going to have to go ahead. From here on in Shaftesbury buries its own dead.

Trinkam: And what are you going to do when our revered chief yells for help . . . ?

As if on key.

Miss Corsa: Mr. Withers on the line.

Thatcher: Hello, Brad? Yes, we're getting things under control. Yes . . . Now, Brad, I'm sure you're looking on the dark side of things. What does Carruthers say? Oh? Yes . . . Well, I'll keep in touch.

Trinkam steps in.

Trinkam: We'd better come in tomorrow to try to clear up the Handasyde report, John.

Thatcher: Yes, Charlie. You hate Saturdays. So it must be really important; alright. Charlie, has it occurred to you that Brad must be having a hell of a time believing that his own sister is a serious suspect.

Trinkam: John, She's in the papers.

Thatcher: A serious suspect? Inescapably, the death of Peggy Lindsay and now of Donald Lindsay was bound up with the divorce of Gilbert and Olivia Austin. But was Olivia the kind of woman . . .?

Thatcher firmly shook his head, and reached for the folder that Trinkam had deposited on his desk. His attention was going to be riveted on matters germane to investment banking.

Trinkam: Specially hard on the Witherses. They've lived like aristocracy, if aristocracy lives well these days. Insulated from most normal human experiences. Hell of a way to take the plunge, isn't it? With murder. Well, I'd appreciate it if you'd read that summary, John.

When the door closed behind her, Thatcher stares idly at the papers before him.

Thatcher mutters again: Trinkam, essentially amoral and nondomestic, put her finger on it. The murders in Shaftesbury were more than a tragedy; they were a revelation. He brought himself up short. Possibly the experience might be a revelation for the Austins. Bradford Withers would escape unscathed; he had his own defenses.

Thatcher continues: Assiduous efforts on Saturday and Sunday should bring the situation under control. I'll have to tell Corsa and Nicolls.

Thatcher: Miss Corsa, I will need you Saturday morning.

No comment. Which made Thatcher grimace.

Nicolls, I'll need you Saturday.

Grimly.

Nicolls: Yes, Sir.

Lincoln Hauser enters by appointment.

Hauser: I expected the worst.

Thatcher: You did?

Hauser: A minimum of publicity. Now look where we are! This thing is completely out of hand.

Thatcher: Yes. Well, Hauser, I suppose you know about this second murder . . .

Hauser: Certainly I do.

Thatcher: The body was found on Withers' place.

Hauser: So the *Journal-American* says. I've already talked to Mr. Withers about it. He wants it all kept out of the papers.

Thatcher: I know you can't do that. But if you can . . .

Hauser: If only I had had a free hand, Thatcher! I can assure you that they could have gone on uncovering bodies in Shaftesbury ad infinitum. I would have had the whole thing under control, if you see what I mean. But—a minimum of publicity! I ask you! What can you do with that?

Thatcher: I admit you were restricted.

Hauser: Restricted! Why, it's like giving Michelangelo some whipped cream and asking him to carve a statue! Oh, I'll do what I can, but frankly, Thatcher, I tell you I'm getting no pleasure out of this job. There's no challenge to creative thinking! It's plodding, unimaginative.

Thatcher let his gaze stray to the *Journal-American*, folded on his desk by Miss Corsa. "Sloan Prexy Detained in Second Murder."

Hauser: There seems to be a good deal for you to get your teeth into.

Hauser: Oh, I'll do my best to calm things down. But—what I could have done! You know, I'm beginning to wonder if the Sloan offers enough scope for a man of more than routine abilities. Not that there's much we can do now! Two murders— and a minimum of publicity!

Thatcher out loud: Fool that he is the publicity is ugly as he read the article.

Blonde Beauty's Brother Second Victim in Connecticut

> October 19, Shaftesbury, Conn. The body of Donald P. Lindsay, brother of Margaret Lindsay, who was murdered here last Sunday, was discovered this morning in the grounds of the estate belonging to Bradford S. Withers. The victim had been beaten to death by blows from a wooden club found lying near the body. Captain Felix T. Parker, State Police Officer in charge of the investigation, reports that Mr. Lindsay was killed between the hours of two o'clock and five o'clock this morning. The discovery was made by Daniel

O'Connell, an employee of Mr. Withers, when he entered the field this morning to move the cattle.

Bradford Withers is President of the Sloan Guaranty Trust in New York and brother of Mrs. Gilbert Austin. Margaret Lindsay and Gilbert Austin were planning to be married after legal termination of the marriage between Mr. Austin and his present wife. Both Mr. and Mrs. Austin have released statements that their contemplated divorce had no bearing on the death of Margaret Lindsay.

Thatcher out loud: They write about the Black Angus being disrupted. I will wager they slept through it, which is more than I could do. Can't help but admire them for it.

Murder Victim Well Known in New York Theatrical Circle

October 20, New York, N.Y.: Donald P. Lindsay, second victim of the crime wave sweeping Shaftesbury, Connecticut, was a familiar figure in the off-Broadway dramatic world. Shortly after graduation from the Yale School of Drama he joined the Little Theatre as assistant stage manager. The Little Theatre in New York's Greenwich Village was a repertory theatre engaged in revivals of the classics, remembered primarily for its presentation of *Oedipus Rex* in modern dress. More recently Mr. Lindsay was associated with the production of Arkansas Richards' *Winter of the Pelican* at the Christopher Street Theatre last winter.

Mr. Richards, interviewed in his New York City apartment this morning, said he spoke for the entire dramatic community in expressing grief and sorrow at the tragedy. Although still young, Donald Lindsay had shown great promise as assistant set designer, and would be mourned by those who had the pleasure of working with him.

A memorial service will be held at the Little Church Around the Corner on next Tuesday.

Back in the office Saturday.

103

Thatcher: Let's get started. At least we can get some work done before Brad calls.

Miss Corsa looks askance; Bowman and Trinkham grin. Phone rings; Thatcher picks up the phone.

Thatcher: Good morning Brad.

Withers V.O.: How did you know it was me. Why can't Hauser keep references about Olivia out of at least *The Times*. We advertise enough.

Thatcher: He's doing his best.

Withers V.O.: He's a fool. And those damned police impounded my antlers and won't release them, John.

Thatcher: Call the Governor. I'm going to have to ring off, Brad.

Thatcher picks up the ringing phone.

Carruthers V.O.: Somebody, unspecified, should try to shut Withers up. He's making things . . . ah, worse.

Thatcher: I understand your feelings because I've been trying to shut him up for decades. I take it you've been up there?

Carruthers V.O.: Just got back.

Thatcher: How bad is it?

Carruthers V.O.: Bad but not terrible.

And rang off.

Thatcher: Let's try to get that Wheeler portfolio cleared up, Nicolls.

The next interruption was from Miss Corsa.

Miss Corsa: Mr. Thatcher there's a call for you from the Governor's office. It's about some antlers.

John Putnam Thatcher gave vent to a long-suppressed explosion of wrath. When he finished, he found his Miss Corsa still waiting.

Thatcher: I apologize for the language, Miss Corsa.

Miss Corsa: Certainly, Mr. Thatcher. About the antlers?

Thatcher: Tell him I'll call back.

Goes home. Comes back in Monday.

Thatcher out loud: Thank God I left the answering machine on Sunday. 4 calls from Withers; 1 from Carruthers; and 1 from George. At least George left a distinct message, "Take care of it the best you can."

Miss Corsa comes in.

You are to call Withers and tell him Mr. Cooke says he has to have Mr. Withers' signature on the Rampollion closing.

Miss Corsa lifts an eyebrow. Thatcher bows to the inevitable.

Alright. Line up the Sloan plane again, Miss Corsa. Presumably now that the Indians are gone we can use it. And tell Gabler to get his files together. He wants Withers' signature too. And Trinkam, for that matter. They're going with me. This bank is going to function if Mr. Withers goes to the penitentiary.

Miss Corsa: And Mr. Nicolls?

Thatcher was at the door of his office.

Thatcher: Nicolls? No, I don't think we'll need him . . .

Miss Corsa: Mr. Thatcher, if you, Ms. Trinkam, Mr. Gabler, and Mr. Withers are in Shaftesbury . . .

Thatcher answers impatiently.

Thatcher: Yes?

. . . and your secretaries are here in New York . . .

Thatcher: Yes?

. . . who is going to run errands for you?

Thatcher grinned suddenly at this uncompromising view of the junior professional staff.

Thatcher: Right as usual, Miss Corsa. And Mr. Nicolls.

## **Chapter 20: Int.-Bar and Restaurant-Day**

Trinkam: Well now that we have flown, been driven to this Inn, and are safely in the bar, I hope no Black Angus joins us. Those howling and yapping dogs are enough.

Thatcher: Charlie, it is a dog show. Hard enough to get the rooms, but you know Miss Corsa. You always become uncomfortable when forced into areas in which the basic living unit is the family. You wince when a station wagon, with an inordinate number of toddlers hanging from its various windows, drives by with no taxis in sight.

They grin together. Gabler looks even grimmer and Nicolls is worn out by it all.

Everett Gabler: Sticking to business as opposed to dogs and cows, I hope to get Withers' signature tonight. I could then Special Delivery the contract to Philadelphia.

Thatcher: Ev, resign yourself to the fact that nothing in Shaftesbury is going to be simple. We've moved here only to try to equalize the Sloan's chances.

Madame Dumont, looking a trifle more tired than she had at last encounter, entered.

Madame Dumont: And, as you see we can give you only these three little rooms, here in the annex. But at least, you are away from the dogs. . . .

Gabler: Nicolls and I can get to work on these papers here and we'll try to get hold of Withers later tonight.

Thatcher out loud: Charlie is set, reaching an understanding with Chef Paul.. Gabler, of course, will do his best to recreate the sixth floor of the Sloan no matter where the wind takes him, but young Nicolls? Well, it will cure him of the mad urge to travel that I have observed in so many young business people. Let him learn that it isn't all expense accounts and skittles.

Madame Dumont: Have you gentlemen dined? Paul Baudelaire is a magnificent chef.

Trinkam: In the bar will be fine. Perhaps he can serve us personally.

Thatcher chuckles, Gabler disapproves, and Nicolls tries to be somewhere else.

Madame Dumont: What a week we have had! First Peggy, then Donald! You cannot imagine the excitement! We have had meetings about it, you understand. But still, Mr. Withers and Olivia insist that we go on with the dog show! But they are no help so it is all left to me. Gil, of course, stays at the Inn and he does what he can with these dog people. But Olivia no! Myself, I think that with two murders, it is not the nicest thing to have a dog show, but they insist . . .

Trinkam: Can't Brad help?

Madame Dumont: Ah, Mr. Withers.

Charlie gets the message and nods, as these bon vivants reach an understanding.

Madame Dumont: Mr. Withers is worried They have the police at Ridge Road Farm all the time. Then there is the *affaire* of the antlers that we will never hear the end of. And in the village, there is bad feeling. People do not like it, you understand, that there are two murders and that nobody knows who killed Peggy or Donald. I do not like it myself, but of course business must go on.

All the bankers nod their approval.

Thatcher: Do the police seriously suspect Olivia?

Madame Dumont: Who knows? But many people do, let me tell you. Since that poor little rat Donald is found murdered on the Withers place, they ask about the fight that Donald had here with Olivia. And they talk about Donald, who ran to the police with the story about his sister. It makes everybody wonder, you see?

Thatcher calls Brad.

Withers V.O.: Thank God you're here. Olivia's here. Listen, John, why don't you come right up? For that matter, why not stay here?

Thatcher: And, it will be easier for me to . . . to coordinate things if I stay here at the Inn.

Withers V.O.: You know best, John. Now, Gabler called me with some damned nonsense about a contract. At a time like this. . . .

Thatcher: It is 4 million, Brad. You'd better see him and sign the thing.

Withers V.O.: Oh, alright! I'll see him at noon tomorrow . . . but John, I want to talk to you.

Thatcher: I'll be up there at nine o'clock tomorrow morning.

On Tuesday morning, John Putnam Thatcher breakfasted very early in the Shaftesbury Inn's pleasantly sunlit bar and restaurant.

Gabler: Charlie isn't down yet.

Thatcher: I didn't expect her to be.

Gabler: Tsk, tsk. Well, once we've got the Flinders papers cleared up, Nicolls and I are going to see Withers at noon; we'll check with Charlie about the annual meeting that Withers wanted to attend. We will put through a call to Walter Bowman.

Everett quaffed a glass of warm water and lemon juice with gusto. Thatcher and Nicolls shudder at the sight.

Gilbert Austin walks in.

Gilbert Austin: Going up to the farm. I'll have to get up to the show in about an hour, but I have to stop at the farm. Do you want a ride?

Thatcher: No. But let's talk for a minute over in the corner..

Gilbert Austin: Want to see Roger. Bold Baron isn't well. We're worried about him. One of our entries . . . then we have this damned kennel tour . . .

Thatcher: Yes.

Gilbert Austin:. . . had to call off the cocktail party, of course. But we still have to take the exhibitors through the Austindale

Kennels on Wednesday. I think that means we have to give them coffee, at least, don't you?

Thatcher: Absolutely.

Gilbert Austin: . . . worried about Bold Baron.

Thatcher: How's Mrs. Lindsay?

Gilbert Austin: She's collapsed. That is, Dr. Cooper says she's alright, but she says that she can't trust herself to get out of bed.

Thatcher: You've seen her?

Gilbert Austin: Of course. It's awkward, you know.

Thatcher: I do indeed..

Gilbert Austin: I mean about Donald wanting to talk to me before he was murdered. It made the police wonder.

Thatcher: No doubt. They heard about it?

Gilbert Austin: Everybody did. Well, I didn't see him and that's all I can say. Do you think that the police seriously suspect Olivia? Giselle was telling me this morning . . .

Thatcher: Yes.

Gilbert Austin: I think that it's time to clear this up. I can't let people go on suffering because I was weak.

Austin leaves.

Thatcher out loud: He sounds rather like his whiny son.

He leaves.

### Scene 21: Int.-Olivia's Living Room-Day

**Gilbert Austin knocks on the door and walks in.**

Withers: Hello Gil. Just talking to Parker. Chief, let's be reasonable about this. We've been cooperative, surely you can't deny that. Now, if only you'd be a little more cooperative . . . Just telling Parker here that I appreciate his difficulties. But I feel that it's only fair to return those antlers. Don't mind for myself, you understand, but they were a gift to Giselle, Madame Dumont, you know, and you know how a man feels . . .

Thatcher walks in.

Chief Parker: The Governor's Office called. I was just explaining to Mr. Withers that we still don't understand why Miss Lindsay was wrapped around them.

Withers: But, you've measured them and photographed them, haven't you? What more do you want?

Gilbert Austin: Excuse the interruption but Parker, is it true that you're seriously concerned about my wife Olivia's story?

Chief Parker: Peggy Lindsay was killed after she had a fight with your wife. A fight that Mrs. Austin claims had nothing to do about the girl's pregnancy. A fight, she says, about the farm. Then, after she denies having seen the girl, the fact slips out, and Donald Lindsay reports it to us. And on Friday night, Donald Lindsay's head was bashed in. Your wife was at home, asleep, alone. Yes, Mr. Austin, we're interested in Mrs. Austin.

Gilbert Austin: You don't believe that Olivia is telling the truth about what she and Peggy were fighting about, is that it?

Bradford Withers was watching his brother-in-law with open-mouthed anxiety.

Chief Parker: I don't say I don't believe it.

Gilbert Austin: I can confirm it. I was there. I saw and heard part of the fight.

Parker looked at him; Thatcher put down his coffee cup.

Withers: Thank God. I saw your car, Gil. I didn't want to say anything but when I was on my way to Winsted, I saw your car parked outside of the farm . . .

Gilbert Austin: Is that why . . . by God! Brad!

Withers: I thought you've been acting strangely. You can't blame me for thinking . . .

Thatcher:: You didn't go inside?

Gilbert Austin: Yes, I wanted to talk to Olivia. I knocked, then I went inside, and there was a fight going on in the living room. Frankly, I just turned on my heel . . .

Withers: Can't blame a man for that.

Thatcher watched Withers exchange a confident smile with Austin.

Captain Parker: I have just a few questions.

Gilbert Austin: Yes? Captain, the fight was extremely unpleasant.

Captain Parker: That's interesting. You confirm your wife's story in all its details, the story she tried to hide, the story you didn't mention earlier. Then Mr. Withers confirms *your* story although he swore earlier that he hadn't seen a thing . . .

Withers: Now look here.

Chief Parker: *And*that would seem to be a neat confirmation of Mrs. Austin's story. Very neat. It's a shame none of you mentioned it earlier. Well, thanks for the coffee Mr. Withers . . .

oh yes, the antlers. We'll probably take them back to the Inn. The Governor can put enough pressure on us to get those antlers back to you. Not much more though.

With this Parthian shot, he exited, bearing, Thatcher conceded, the honors.

Withers: What did he mean by that?

Gilbert Austin: Lying.

Withers: Good God!

## Scene 22: Int.-Bar and Restaurant-Day

Trinkam: It's a mess. I tried to talk to Withers this afternoon but he had that kid with him.

Nicolls speaks gloomily.

Nicolls: Bud.

Trinkam: It would be. Couldn't get near him. So I just slipped away and improved the afternoon . . .

Ken smirks to himself.

Everett Gabler: I managed to get Withers' signature on the Flinders contract. It's on its way to Philadelphia. It wasn't easy . . .

Thatcher looked at him inquiringly.

I can't convince myself that Withers had the slightest idea of what he was signing.

Thatcher: Probably didn't, Ev, through no fault of your own, mind you.

Gabler: Withers.. There's something a little evasive about him.

Thatcher: He was, it develops, lying about having seen nothing the afternoon of Peggy Lindsay's death. He saw Gil Austin's car on Ridge Road. in a way it's a comfort. I was afraid he might be involved with some imbecility with Madame that would make our lot with the tabloids even harder . . .

Trinkam: Withers and Giselle?

Thatcher: Yes, why?

Trinkam: Waste. Sheer waste. She needs a man of wide experience.

Thatcher: You're thinking of someone like Gilbert Austin, I take it.

Trinkam: I was not.

Gabler: I can see that we're going to get a lot of work done. Murders! Divorces! And to top it all these dog people!

Trinkam: What they need is some Fair Trade legislation. Giselle has been telling me about the talk about price cutting, just like department stores complaining about discounters. Enlightening.

Thatcher: I don't expect the discount houses will enter the field for some time.

Gabler: You never know. John, it is a much bigger business, and a growing one, than I imagined. We should keep an eye on it; but if Bowman finds out we may wind up owning too much.

Trinkam: Oh, come on, Everett, cheer up. If we have any free time, I'm going to take in the Doberman show tomorrow morning. It's always nice to have a change in pace.

Gabler: Hmph! I suppose that's what you were fixing up with Chef Paul.

Trinkam: That's right. Will beat Bowman to the punch on this one. Paul has promised to explain the workings of dog shows to me. After all, you never know, we may want to underwrite a kennel some time.

Gabler: I thought you were eager to get Withers' OK on the Handasyde report.

Trinkam; Nicolls can handle it. If I get tied up, that is.

Charlie grins; Everett snorts.

Thatcher: You two seem to be having your usual good time, although you did agree on the dog business. Tamer, eh? Did you get Brad to read the Amesbury estimates, Everett?

Gabler: I did not! I was lucky to get his signature. He didn't have the time to do a single thing more. So, tomorrow . . .

Thatcher got up and shook himself. The dogs were influencing everyone.

Thatcher muttered: Nice to have the bar to ourselves as they have their own place in the dining room. The trip has worked out pretty well; Trinkam can handle the documents with both arms tied behind her back; picked up a new expertise in her own idiosyncratic way; Gabler kept everyone up to form; Nicolls was aging like good wine. And having Withers in Connecticut was a lot easier place to get a signature than on some mountain in Asia or safari in Africa.

He raised his glass and saluted the town. Then Roger Kincaid burst in with a Mr. Oldfield in tow.

Roger Kincaid: Oldfield, I want a word with you.

Oldfield: You looking for me, Kincaid? I tell you I'm a little busy right now. If it can wait . . .

Roger Kincaid: It can't..

Oldfield: Now just a minute, Kincaid . . .

Roger Kincaid: Never mind that. I've got something to settle and we're going to settle it right now. Who's started all this filthy talk about Bold Baron having distemper?

Oldfield: Distemper! Good God, I had no idea. Why I didn't even know that you had it at your kennel.

Roger Kincaid: We don't.

Oldfield. Who the hell do you think you're talking to? And what do you mean letting a Dog Show come to a town that's infected? I'm going out to tell the others.

Bartender: Well that's the end of that tour. Seen it before.

And it was.

The Bankers looked on mystified.

Thatcher: I gather that distemper is contagious.

Trinkam: Highly. One of the greatest hazards in dog breeding. The really terrible thing about it is that human beings, although they don't get it, can carry it. They're developing vaccines against it but they're not perfected. As the barkeep said, that's the end of the tour.

## Chapter 23: Int.-Bar and Restaurant-Day

Thatcher: As famously said, the starry-eyed utopianism of Americans can keep them butting up their heads against the wall, but when you push executives to the wall, they are likely to read the handwriting on it. So we have to move out of this field of dry wells, Brad Withers, and move on.

116

Trinkam: Quite right. To get Withers focused on getting contracts signed, to get reports cleared, in short, to transact business, is seems doomed now, even here. John, what do you think? Ev?

Gabler: Charlie's right. There's no use wasting more time here, John. I called Withers this morning and it's clearly out of the question to try to get anything more out of him.

Nicolls just nodded, making it unanimous. Gabler continued.

It was only to be expected that two murders in which Withers, or his sister or her husband, are implicated . . ."

This reminded Thatcher of his duties to the Sloan. He interrupts.

Thatcher: Everett, things are bad enough. Our line is feudal loyalty in the teeth of the evidence.

Gabler: At any rate, deteriorations were to be expected. I don't approve of them, but I understand them . . .

Trinkam: But Everett, the Flinders contract is OK. It's the damned Handasyde report that's being held up.

Gabler: What I do not understand, I say, is why the illness of a Doberman pinscher should be allowed to bring essential bank business to a halt, especially after we have all come here to Connecticut to accommodate Withers. No doubt, Charlie, you can enlighten us.

Trinkam: What was that? Missed what you were saying, Everett.

Thatcher left for the phone booth to call Brad, muttering to himself.

117

Thatcher out loud: Nevertheless, there was something in what Gabler said as there usually is. Brad, need you to sign some papers.

Withers V.O.: Too busy with all this.

Thatcher: We will be up this afternoon.

And hung up. Thatcher emerged from the telephone booth to find his subordinates eyeing him hopefully.

We're going to have to sit this out. We'll take this morning off and we'll tackle Brad this afternoon . . .

Trinkam: OK.

Gabler cast a disgruntled look after her.

Gabler: Nicolls and I will refresh our knowledge of the details of the Handasyde report.

Nicolls gave Thatcher a plea for escape.

Thatcher: I'll need Nicolls.

Gabler: Fine.

Gabler leaves.

Thatcher: Well, if nothing else, Nicolls, we can find out how the Sloan is getting along without us. Do you have any change? Miss Corsa? Thank God.

Miss Corsa V.O.: We are fine here, Mr. Thatcher.

Thatcher: There is no need to be offensive. I suppose that Bowman is losing his mind over those trucking stocks now that there's nobody there to hold him down.

Miss Corsa V.O.: We bought 40,000 shares, yesterday.

Thatcher: Good Lord! Now Miss Corsa, I want Bowman to call me before he plunges the whole Investment Division into chaos. I want you to make that clear to him . . .

Miss Corsa V.O.: Certainly, Mr. Thatcher. And Mr. Hauser. . .

Thatcher: That insufferable ass.

 Miss Corsa reprovingly.

Gabler: We never had any of this at Swarthmore.

Miss Corsa V.O.: He has a resignation ready. But he wants to know whom he should send it to.

 Thatcher deflated by the reproving.

Thatcher: Me. Thank you Miss Corsa.

 Everyone leaves Thatcher alone. Banker Green walks in, looking again like a banker on vacation. Thatcher smiles.

Green: Heard you were here; tired of it; came in for a pop, as we used to say.

Thatcher: Indeed, let's both have one.

Green: Quite a little business isn't it, these dogs. As a small time banker in Portland, not like the Sloan, we have financed a few kennels. Real money makers; small land required; nearby customers have money; and pick em up and pay cash on the barrelhead. Have several now. Would like more customers like that. $1500 for the right pup.

Thatcher: What? $1500 per?

 Green looks at him.

Green: As a banker, I am on the low side of course. Some of the fancier kennels and some of the popular breeds go higher. And for an outstanding champion, the price can go a lot higher than that.

Thatcher: That makes last night's scene clearer to me.

Green: You mean about the distemper? That's why they all have heavy insurance; we require that on loans, payable to us, of course.

Thatcher: I had not realized that it was also a major financial threat.

Green: For a lot of us dogs are a hobby; but for a lot of people here dogs are business, a big business sometimes like with at the Austin kennels.

Thatcher: Why didn't anybody object to Gilbert Austin's continuing here as business manager? Surely he can transmit the disease?

Green: Well, in the first place, who would do the work? Then, the chances of his transmitting distemper are fairly remote. He hasn't been at the Austindale Kennels lately, you know. Then, nobody wants to add to the troubles he already has. There's been a lot of talk about Peggy Lindsay's murder. Most of the people here knew her fairly well, you know. But Gil Austin is a pretty popular guy, and nobody wants to make it hard for him.

Thatcher: Could this rumor about distemper be just that, nothing more than a rumor? Something that one of the competitors of the Austindale Kennels started to keep them from showing?

Green: Let's put it this way: nine out of ten people here wouldn't do a thing like that . . .

Thatcher: But the tenth?

Green: It wouldn't surprise me out of a year's growth.

Thatcher: It is always a pleasure to meet a banker.

And they both grinned at each other.

## Chapter 24: Int.-Bar and Restaurant-Night

Thatcher relaxes at his table with Nicolls. Charlie and Chef Paul stop by. Madame Dumont enters.

Thatcher: Charlie, I've been looking for Austin. Have you seen him anywhere? He's clearly not at bar.

Trinkam: No, haven't seen him.

Madame Dumont: Poor Gilbert. He works all the day at the dog show, and tonight he will also work, and now, he cannot relax. No, he must go up to have the discussions with the state veterinarian.

Thatcher: Oh. Gone up to the farm, has he?

Madame Dumont: Yes. And it is hard for him. Olivia . . . Olivia is not kind.

Thatcher: I'm eager to see this vet. Seems to be a peculiar and little known branch of the civil service.

Trinkam: I don't want to raise your hopes, John, but it's either the vets or the AMA descending right now, looking out the window.

Gilbert comes in with Olivia a discrete distance behind him with a man with each.

Gilbert Austin: Not the slightest doubt. Dr. Mallory will be here to tell you so himself. He has already told us that he doesn't see how this rumor could have got started.

From across the room he was ably seconded by his wife.

Olivia Austin: Obviously someone who doesn't know the first thing about distemper symptoms. We wanted you to know that you could all be easy in your own minds.

Dr. Mallory enters.

Dr. Mallory: Just wanted to say hello. Will have a quick drink and then tell the crowd.

Dr. Mallory leaves with a smile at each Austin and a grin. Bud enters and speaks to Thatcher.

Bud Austin: It's pretty silly, all this fuss about dogs. He fixed his companion with a baleful eye.

Thatcher said in a voice that had intimidated many an MBA and junior executive.

Thatcher: Young man, when you are a good deal older and wiser you will realize that no event which makes adults feel this good is silly.

Bud leaves abruptly.

Gilbert Austin: Good for you. I've been waiting two weeks for someone to tell him he's a brat. I should have of course.

Roger wanders in for a drink. Cynthia follows him.

Roger Kincaid: That's my girl. A great dog with a great future.

Trinkam and Chef Paul go over to Olivia. Madame Dumont joins them.

Olivia Austin: Nice to be here to see things, Giselle. You did a wonderful job.

Giselle blossoms in the flattery..

Gil Austin: You don't have to raise beef to lose money, Tim. Dogs will do.

His companion laughs. Fundheim walks in and starts to talk to Roger.

Fundheim: I'd like to see the kennel tomorrow, Roger. It was promised to get us here.

Roger Kincaid: The tour was postponed.

Fundheim: I don't see what difference the day makes.

Roger Kincaid: I expect you don't know our problems, Fundheim. We've got a couple of murders to cope with, a farm going to hell, and a sick dog. We don't have time for guided tours.

Fundheim: Then you shouldn't make indiscriminate invitations.

Cynthia Kincaid: Oh, for heaven's sake, Roger. I'll show him the kennel.

Roger Kincaid: Like hell you will! You've got too much to do already. Look, we expected to exhibit a fine lot of Dobermans. So we've all got our disappointments.

Cynthia Kincaid: But what difference . . .

Roger Kincaid: Don't you understand English? We're not showing the kennel. I'm sick and tired of a . . . of . . .

He lurched unsteadily to his feet, drunker, Thatcher saw, than he had first appeared.

Cynthia Kincaid: Of course, Roger. Do you want to come outside with me for a bit?

He follows her out.

Fundheim, about to pursue the subject, was quelled into silence by Roger's final comment over his shoulder.

Roger Kincaid: It's final, you hear.

Madame Dumont: Poor Roger. When he drinks, his temper becomes undependable.

Mr. Fundheim looked rather frightened. Gilbert nods.

Gilbert Austin: John, Cynthia will take care of him. He'll be alright in the morning.

In the main dining room they could hear cheering and then singing. Thatcher went out to join them with a smile.

## Chapter 25. Int.-Bar and Restaurant-Night

Nicolls and Gabler breakfasting.

Gabler: A disgrace to the Sloan. These . . . these peccadillos, I suppose we may call them . . . are certainly a violation of the canon of ethics of the American Bankers Association. Charlie's notable tango with Chef Paul at one point in last night's proceedings was appalling.

Nicolls: It was something wasn't it with Mr. Thatcher's spirited rendition of *Crimson in Triumph Flashing*? Harvard! Harvard! Harvard! Harvard! Harvard! Harvard! HAR-VARD!! And then Mr. Withers' counter with rival and appropriate claims, finished off by Bulldog! Bulldog! Bow Wow Wow!

Gabler: We never had any of this at Swarthmore.

Gabler snorts and get ready to leave. Thatcher walks in, the picture of health and well-being.

Thatcher: Everett, on your way up to Withers? Good luck to you.

Gabler finally leaves the room with an even more censorious look.

Oh, Nicolls. I believe I recall suggesting you as a speaker to the Black Angus Cooperative Society last night. You may have to do something about it.

You know, Nicolls, Napoleon was right: the best defense is attack. You look aggrieved; that will pass with age.

Mutters out loud: I feel so reconciled to Shaftesbury, the dog show, and the world in general, that I will join the hero of last night's festivities, Dr. Mallory, the state veterinarian.

Dr. Mallory: Nice to have you join me. Beautiful place, Shaftesbury,.

Thatcher: It is. Do you get around much in your job?

Dr. Mallory: The state veterinarian's office was a fascinating place to work. If it wasn't mastitis in New Haven, it was the threat of psitticosis in Hartford. Keeps me on the go.

Thatcher: And hoof-and-mouth disease?

Dr. Mallory: Not in Shaftesbury. These Black Anguses are pampered, petted. . . . Let me tell you, Thatcher, if the people of Connecticut were treated as well as these Black Anguses, this would be a happier world.

Thatcher: What about the Dobermans? Surely those Dobermans are just as pampered and yet there was this danger of distemper.

Dr. Mallory: In a way you're right, Thatcher. I don't deny it. There was Bold Baron. But how anybody could have thought it was distemper, I do not understand.. They've got a beautiful kennel with all the latest improvements. Kincaid knows his business. You know, as a realistic businessman . . .

Thatcher braces himself.

As a realistic businessman, I think I would suspect an Austindale competitor. Those are beautiful creatures up there.

Fundheim: Morning! Mind if I join you?

Pause while he pours coffee.

Wanted to see Austindale. But I guess I'll start home. I understand they've got those new inside blowers.

Dr. Mallory: Oh, they do.

The door opened. A policeman was there with the antlers, with Chief Parker behind him. Madame Dumont came in from the other door.

Madame Dumont: What are you doing with those now? Never do I want to see them again. When I close my eyes, I see poor Peggy.

Chief Parker ignores her.

Chief Parker: Put it down over there, Dooley.

Dooley staggers over to the table and deposits his burden.

Madame Dumont: No, I do not want it. It reminds me.

Chief Parker: Lady. This is an important bit of evidence. We still don't know why Peggy Lindsay was jammed into it when she was killed in your Inn.

Madame Dumont: Now, really . . .

Chief Parker: . . . and we would like to hold on to it. But Mr. Bradford Withers is a friend of the Senator, a friend of the

Governor, a friend of the Mayor. He wants you to have it, and when you've got friends like that. . .

Gabler stomps in with Nicolls in tow.

Gabler: Wild-goose chase. Brad's not home.

Thatcher: You surprise me. I expected that he would still be in bed. Oh, Nicolls. It appears that I did not commit you to the Black Angus Cooperative Society. Dr. Mallory said I committed some other poor soul.

Nicolls closes his eyes in a brief prayer of gratitude for blessings rendered. Gabler slams some papers on the table, glares down at the majestic antlers and says,

Gabler: Dammit, this whole thing is impossible. First Charlie…

Trinkam enters.

Trinkam: Good morning, all!

Gabler: Withers' houseboy said he got a telegram. And he dashed out. Seems Mrs. Withers is due to arrive. Now John, Charlie's Handasyde report has got to be cleared. I suggest we go back to New York this afternoon.

Madame Dumont: Again, I do not care who knows Mr. Withers. These antlers, I do not want.

Chief Parker: Listen, when the Governor calls . . .

Gabler: At the Sloan we can get Lancer's signature.

Outside there was suddenly a brawl with dogs, people, and two smashed cars. Everyone looked out. When the rumpus was over, they walk away from the windows.

Madame Dumont: I'm tired of dogs. Very tired. No doubt I will have to house the dogs whose owners are in jail. And I am tired of antlers, as well, I tell you. Look at them. How ugly.

They looked. There on the long table were Everett Gabler's unread papers. But of antlers, there was no sign at all.

Everett Gabler: John, I'm going to want to talk to you.

Thatcher: Not now.

One look at Thatcher made Gabler back off.

Everett Gabler: Well, I'll try to find Withers then.

Gabler leaves. Trinkam and Nicolls retire to a distant table.

Captain Parker: What do you mean, stolen? Where are they . . . ?

Madame Dumont: Look. When we are out looking at those dogs. Somebody comes in, no doubt a madman, and takes them. It is easy . . .

Suddenly she broke off.

Chief Parker: Why would anybody want to steal them? Tell me that!

Giselle did not seem to hear him.

Thatcher mutters to himself: It is clear now and Giselle seems to get it too. Brad needs those antlers in the house before Carrie gets home. And he did it while everyone was distracted, just like at the parade with a body.

Thatcher out loud: Of course. She wasn't killed at the Inn at all. She never got to the Inn. Somebody made it look that way.

128

Captain, I'd like a few words with you.

Chief Parker looks at Thatcher, breaks off with Madame Dumont, and follows him to a corner.

Madame Dumont: He too, he knows.

Charlie Trinkam: What is this?

Giselle looks at him, then without another word left the room.

Thatcher: So that's the story Captain. Roger Kincaid did it. He won't protest when you arrest him.

He didn't.

## Chapter 26: Int.-Thatcher's Office-Day

Nicoll, Trinkam, Gabler, and Thatcher are in conference.

Trinkam: What about the tax credits?

Everyone paused.

Well I would say the high point of the trip was Everett and his dog riding back with us.

Gabler: I admit the Welsh Terrier. Llewellyn ap Llandanagh. Remarkable blood lines..

Charlie snorted. Miss Corsa enters.

Miss Corsa: Mr. Thatcher, Mrs. Withers is here for you.

Thatcher: Show him in.

Miss Corsa: *Mrs.* Withers. She would like to see you.

Thatcher: Of course, of course.

Thatcher muttering: Carrie is the most detached and probably most intelligent of the group, so I'll try to explain it again.

Carrie Withers (65 elegant and aggressive): I know I'm interrupting, John, but I couldn't leave without thanking you for all your help in Shaftesbury.

Thatcher: It was nothing. Brad had never been a serious suspect.

Carrie Withers: Oh, that's not what I mean. But you stopped him from making more of a fool of himself. Or anyway as much as possible.

The others made movements to leave..

No, no, you mustn't go. I'm grateful to all of you. And you're Ms. Trinkam. Chef Paul has told me all about you.

Charlie, a woman of wide experience, contented herself with a cheerful grin.

And of course I want to hear all about the goings on too. Roger Kincaid! I could hardly believe it when Brad told me. Why in the world should Roger go around killing the Lindsays?

Thatcher: Money.

Carrie Withers: But Roger doesn't have any money. Neither do the Lindsays.

Thatcher: No, Roger doesn't have any money in the Shaftesbury scheme of things. That's what confused things all along. The Shaftesbury view of life.

Carrie looks bewildered.

Carrie Withers: What do you mean by that?

Thatcher: Shaftesbury thinks in terms of capital and tax losses. So we all accepted two facts which were completely untrue. First, the Kincaids, Roger a farm manager and Cynthia a minister's daughter, have no money. They just happen to live like the rest of Shaftesbury. And second, all farming in Shaftesbury is unprofitable. That's its chief purpose.

Carrie Withers: What do you mean, live like the rest of Shaftesbury? Why, the Kincaids don't have a place!

Thatcher: No, Carrie, but they just happen to send their children to the same schools as Shaftesbury, drive the same cars as Shaftesbury, and take part in the social life of Shaftesbury. On top of all that, Roger is a drinker, which happens to be a very expensive habit. You don't do any of that on a farm manager's salary. Good heavens, if a teller in one of the Sloan offices did any of that, we'd have his books audited instantly! But in the atmosphere of Shaftesbury, if you're not raising prize beef at a loss, you're maintaining the standard of living of a working man.

Trinkam: Now, there is where Kincaid used his head. Capitalizing on loss farming in a totally new way.

Carrie Withers: You can't tell me that anybody could raise beef in Connecticut at a profit. That's not possible!

Thatcher: Of course not. But the reason you can't is because commercial beef ranching requires large tracts of cheap pasture land. You go to Texas for that, not suburban Connecticut. The Austins were so indoctrinated with that concept that they never stopped to ask themselves why that reasoning should apply to raising Doberman pinschers. It doesn't. You buy the same feed for your kennel no matter where you are. The Austindale Kennel was being run at a very handsome profit and it was all going into Roger Kincaid's pocket.

Carrie Withers: Brad didn't explain that.

This surprised no one.

Nicolls: You have to hand it to Peggy Lindsay, figuring all this out.

Thatcher: Yes. The contemplated marriage between Gilbert Austin and Peggy was a deathblow to Kincaid. No wonder he was so upset by the divorce and worked so hard for a reconciliation! The last thing in the world he wanted was to have Peggy Lindsay around Ridge Road Farm.

Carrie Withers: But she'd already been around. She used to show some of the Dobermans.

Thatcher: She'd been around as a handler earning a fee on a piecework basis. Now suddenly she was taking on an ownership interest. You've got to remember that Peggy Lindsay was as much of a wage earner as Roger Kincaid. And what was much more dangerous, her business was dogs. I noticed very early that while Gil and Olivia referred to Ridge Road Farm as the house or my home, Peggy always called it the property. And I made the mistake of attributing this to the difference in moneyed status.

Giselle Dumont said some sensible things to me the night of the murder. She said we all thought of Peggy as the 'other woman' when really she was an acute businesswoman. But I was too blind to see the implications. When Peggy said property, she meant it. She didn't see a house, she saw an income-producing kennel. Of course, she wanted the house too, and for all the reasons Olivia mentioned. But what infuriated her was Olivia trying to hold on to the house by denying the value of the business.

Gabler: Then she didn't know Roger Kincaid was in back of it?

Thatcher: Not at first she didn't. From what Kincaid has told in his confession, it's pretty clear that her awareness didn't come to her until the last day.

Nicolls: Oh, has Kincaid confessed?

Thatcher: Oh, yes. He was never built to be a premeditated murderer, you know. He just had fallen into the lifelong habit of taking the easy way out. When he drank too much for city life, he moved to the country. When he couldn't make as much money in the country, he stole. When somebody found him out, he murdered.

Trinkam: Peggy. You were telling us about how she found out about Kincaid.

Thatcher: That's simple enough. She went up to have her big scene with Olivia at Ridge Road Farm. While she was screaming denunciations at Olivia, it came over her that Gil and Olivia were genuinely innocent of the money-making qualities of their kennel. And Gil was just as much in the dark as Olivia.

Olivia had roused her to a white-hot pitch of fury in the course of their quarrel, and she was always a girl who flung herself at things when she was worked up enough to overcome her basic lack of self-confidence. You know what happened next. She realized that the profits had been diverted before they ever reached the Austins and flung out of the house, leaving Olivia in mid-sentence, to have it out with Roger. Remember, Cynthia said she was boiling with rage when she passed the Kincaid house. So she was. Roger in his first statement just pushed her farther along the road to the village. Of course she was murdered right there. Roger says he had no idea of what he was doing and I believe him. She charged up to Roger, still in fury, and started abusing him as a thief, stealing from her Gil. Roger, who had been living on his nerves for days anyway while Peggy complained loud and long to the entire village about the valuation of Ridge Road Farm, just lost control and struck her. The next thing he knew he had a body with a broken neck slumped over the barbed wire in his field.

Trinkam: Barbed wire. So that's how the antlers got involved.

Thatcher: Exactly.

Nicolls: Now just a moment. I don't see that at all.

Thatcher: You've got to put yourself in Kincaid's position. There he was with a body that couldn't possibly have acquired a broken neck accidentally in its present position. So he had to move it. All he really wanted to do was find some place in the fields with a hill and rocks and briars where the marks on the body could reasonably be explained. Particularly the damage done by the barbed wire getting entangled with Peggy's arms. So he loaded the body on the back of the pickup truck he had in the field with him, covered it with a tarp, and was about to set off when Cynthia appeared, demanding that he immediately drive to the parade. There wasn't anything he could do but drive into town, drop his family, and then go about his disposal activities. It was at this point that the antlers entered the picture.

Carrie frowning mightily.

Carrie Withers: I'm interested in those antlers.

Thatcher: Brad wanted them at the Inn for the dinner that night. He was just ahead of Kincaid in the traffic jam by the village green. Roger, you realize, was just about frantic by that time. He didn't really dare leave the truck for a minute with that tarp loosely concealing its contents. Then what does he see? The entire staff of the Inn out front and Brad depositing the antlers inside and then going off to the parade. He just drove around back and walked in with the body. We all saw the other day that when everybody's attention is riveted on some spectacle on the village green, you can walk in and out of the back of the Inn carrying anything you want and nobody will notice.

As soon as Kincaid got the idea to leave the body draped around the antlers, he realized it would be to his benefit to make it seem that Peggy had been killed at the Inn. So he left her purse and gloves in the front hall. He had to get rid of them anyway. Then, in a moment of inspiration, he took the place

134

cards out of her purse and put them around the dining room. He was careful to separate the Lindsay-Austin factions, but didn't pay much attention to anything else. That's how I ended up with the garden enthusiasts. Actually he didn't get back to Cynthia until the last section of the parade was passing. All the business at the Inn took some time. He could have parked in much less than half an hour.

Carrie Withers: And Donald Lindsay? I suppose it was the same thing that Peggy figured out.

Thatcher: Yes, but Roger didn't give him as long to work on it. Donald was used to thinking of his sister in economic terms and he was sure that money was in back of her murder. That may have been good sense but personally I think it was congenital bias. Anyway, he clearly intended to keep things stirred up, probably in the hope that he could exist on blackmail in the future. He put pressure on everyone and by the time he made a few significant remarks to Roger about the valuation of Ridge Road Farm, Roger agreed to meet him at night. You recall that Roger was sitting up those nights with Bold Baron. When he met him, he killed him.

Nicolls: My God, I actually sat and watched him hose off the pickup truck!

Thatcher smiles grimly.

Thatcher: Yes, Roger Kincaid had plenty of troubles after the murder. With the police continually tramping around the Austin place, he had to undertake his cleanup operations in the blaze of publicity. I sat and saw him remove the section of barbed wire against which Peggy Lindsay fell. But barbed wire isn't easy to dispose of. Particularly in a countryside where no one else uses it. The police found that section he removed in the shed. There were still fragments of Peggy's tweed jacket and dried blood on it.

135

Carrie Withers: What's all this about the distemper rumor? Brad said he could believe Roger might commit a murder but not that he could slander the Austindale Kennel.

Three bankers sat in respectful silence. The fourth was more responsive.

Gabler: Disgraceful.

Thatcher: That's what I meant about Roger having plenty of other problems. Much against his wishes, Gil and Olivia foisted a dog show in Shaftesbury on him and then invited all the participants to a kennel tour. With everybody speculating about possible motives for Peggy Lindsay's murder, he certainly did not want some 60 dog experts wandering around his kennel making loud estimates of its profitability. Kincaid would know that you could count on their talking nothing but dogs and kennel profits throughout their stay. So he went to work. The first thing he did was act as peacemaker between Giselle Dumont and Olivia Austin and have the cocktail party at Ridge Road Farm cancelled.

But that wasn't enough for his purposes. So he did a very obvious thing. He went down to the Inn when he knew it would be crowded with exhibitors and demanded to know who had started a rumor of distemper with a great show of righteous indignation. Remember, nobody had ever seen him so upset before? Now, you know what kind of furor was caused by the word 'distemper.' Is it likely that there could have been a rumor before Roger started it? Of course not. We would have had people howling for the state vet. So at one blow, Roger accomplished two things. He got the kennel tour called off in such a way that no one would come near the place, and he got the Austindale Kennels disbarred from the ring. A very economical operation.

Trinkam: And when did you catch on to this?

Thatcher: Nothing was clear until Brad walked off with the antlers and I realized how easy it would have been to bring a body into the Inn. But I think I began to wonder the night before. Gil said something about it's being as easy to lose money on dogs as on beef and that didn't make sense. Then there was Roger's display with that miserable little exhibitor who wanted to upset all Kincaid's plans by going up to the kennel the next day. For an easygoing man Kincaid was remarkably offensive.

Trinkam: He was drunk, you know. . . After all, we were all a little sozzled.

Thatcher: There's drunk and there's drunk. Everyone was a little tipsy, true. But Roger acted as if he were drunk enough to be taken home by his wife. Drunk enough to become disagreeably quarrelsome. Then we are told he's a problem drinker. Now a good practiced, hardened drinker doesn't become heavily drunk to the point of slurring his words and reeling on his feet when everybody else is mildly tipsy. No, Roger was putting on a show. And for a very good reason, too.

Carrie Withers: Really extraordinary. It hardly seems possible that we can all settle back to the same old lives in Shaftesbury, now.

Thatcher involuntarily raises an eyebrow.

Carrie Withers: John. It took me about ten minutes to fix *that* up.

This was instantly intelligible to Thatcher and Trinkam, incomprehensible to Nicolls, and uninteresting to Gabler who was sneaking surreptitious glances at "Showing Your Own Dog."

Carrie Withers: Men are such fools.

Trinkam nodded with a smile; the men did not have the temerity to comment.

Thatcher: Everything is alright?

Carrie Withers: Well of course it is. I sympathize with Olivia, of course. But years ago I warned her that marrying a Quaker was going to be no bed of roses . . .

Thatcher: Carrie, will you please tell me what Olivia was so angry about? It's the one thing that eludes me.

Carrie Withers: Why, Gil's perfectly asinine behavior, of course. For heaven's sake, John. Here she is, her life totally disrupted, she didn't go to Paris this year, you know, because Gil wanted a divorce. . . .

Thatcher: Yes, I understood that much.

Carrie Withers: I doubt it. Well, of course Olivia was wonderful about it. Naturally she wondered what the man saw in poor Peggy Lindsay . . .

Thatcher: Naturally.

Carrie bleated sarcastically, diamonds flashing.

Carrie Withers: But of course Olivia's a great romantic, you know, so she told herself that Gil was in love. At his age! Hah!

Thatcher: Why did she get so upset, then, when she heard about the baby?

Carrie Withers: Well, how would you feel? She discovered that Gil proposed to disrupt a perfectly happy home, to drag them through the divorce courts *not* because he was desperately in love, but simply because he felt the gentlemanly thing to do was to marry Peggy Lindsay! Really! Olivia hadn't really grasped what I meant about Quakers, you see. She was utterly outraged by this . . . juvenile attitude!

Thatcher: And?

Carrie Withers: I had a long talk with each of them. And I made Gil promise never to stray again. He won't of course. He's not really the type. All of this was a mistake at the Canandaigua Dog Show, I understand. But it makes him feel better to think he's undergoing a penance of some sort. Particularly when he feels so wretched about Roger.

Thatcher: Has anybody succeeded in convincing him of Kincaid's guilt?

Carrie Withers: Oh, Roger didn't make any bones about it when Gil went to see him. But Gil was always very fond of Roger so now he's managed to convince himself that somehow he's responsible. It's just the sort of thing he would do. I'm sure that poor Peggy never had any idea that Gil didn't want to marry her. He would have made it a point to hide his feelings from her. Really, he is perfectly infuriating. Or, he would be if he weren't so attractive.

Thatcher: And Olivia? Is she wretched about Kincaid too?

Carrie Withers: Olivia, is far too happy to think about anybody but Gil. Real happiness, you know, is a very selfish business. She even promised me that . . .

Thatcher: What in the world did you make her give up?

Carrie smiles.

Carrie Withers: Just a few of her cultural activities. A man can take just so much polished perfection. Actually, in spite of everything, they're happy as children to be together again. They're taking off for the Bahamas, it will do them good to get away from Shaftesbury . . .

Thatcher: Splendid.

Carrie Withers: Oh, that would have never come to anything. Giselle doesn't have much patience.

Nicolls: And Mr. Withers has back that fine stag head he shot, so everything's alright.

Carrie stiffened into a figure of outrage.

Carrie Withers: The head that *who* shot?

Nicolls: But Mr. Withers . . .

Carrie Withers: Do you mean to tell me that Brad has had the gall to maintain that he shot that stag? The stag that I stalked for four hours? He's been going around saying . . . Well, I'm going to have it out with him right now!

She roars out without another word.

Nicolls: It's not that important who shot those antlers.

There was a moment of heavy silence. Thatcher says gently

Thatcher: I don't think, Nicolls, that you've fully absorbed the Shaftesbury view of these things.

Made in United States
North Haven, CT
14 May 2023

36583482R00086